MONSTERSTREET

THE BOY WHO CRIED WEREWOLF

1

MONSTERSTREET

THE BOY WHO CRIED WEREWOLF

J. H. REYNOLDS

 KATHERINE TEGEN BOOKS
An Imprint of HarperCollins Publishers

Katherine Tegen Books is an imprint of
HarperCollins Publishers.

Monsterstreet #1: The Boy Who Cried Werewolf
Copyright © 2019 by J. H. Reynolds

Library of Congress Control Number: 2018965101
ISBN 978-0-06-286935-7 (trade bdg.)
ISBN 978-0-06-286934-0 (pbk.)

Typography by Ray Shappell
19 20 21 22 23 PC/LSCH 10 9 8 7 6 5 4 3 2 1
❖
First Edition

To Mom, Dad, and Sis.
For an amazing childhood.

To my dear wife, Rebekah.
None of my books would exist without you.

And to my little darlings, Lily Belle and Poet Eve.
You give meaning to everything.

1

NO SERVICE

The dirt road twisted through the forest like a snake, but the scrawny boy in the passenger seat didn't notice. His shaggy hair and brown eyes were veiled by a red hoodie as he stared down at his iPad, annihilating monsters on some faraway planet.

Suddenly, the cell bars at the top of the screen vanished, and the game froze.

"No service?" The boy shook the device, trying to wake the dead.

"You'll survive for a couple of days, Max," his mother said, driving their blue minivan deeper into the woods. "When I was twelve, we didn't have all those distractions—we played outside. It will just take some time to get used to being away from the city."

Max sank into his seat and sighed.

He looked out his window, and saw the tall, prickly pine trees for the first time. On the side of the road, he glimpsed a rusted metal sign that read, *Now Entering Wolf County. Population 781.* Oddly, the number "781" had been crossed out with red spray paint, and "634" had been written in its place.

"Creepyville," Max mumbled, then turned to his mom. "Do I really have to stay out here the whole weekend?"

It was more of a plea than a question.

"We've already been over this, honey," his mother replied. "I swear, you're just like your father—always questioning things. That's what made him a good scientist, I suppose."

"But I've never even met these people. And now you want me to stay with them by myself for three days?"

"You've met them before. You just don't remember," she said. "In fact, we lived out here for a while when you were a baby. Before—"

She paused, and there was an awkward moment of silence. Max knew she was about to refer to his father's accidental death, but it was something she rarely said aloud. He had asked her about it more times than he could count, but she always found a way to change the subject before he could get any real answers. In fact, he hardly knew anything about his father.

"Believe me, Max, this is the last place on earth I want to be," his mother said, tapping the steering wheel. She had been acting strangely toward him the past few days. "If you want to know the truth, your gramps and grammy wrote me a letter on your birthday asking for you to come stay with them this weekend. They seemed rather urgent about it. Said they have some things of your father's that they want to pass down to you. It was supposed to be a surprise."

Max still wasn't convinced.

"Why haven't they ever come to our house? And why is this the first time we've gone to see them?"

His mother took a deep breath.

"You're getting older now, and I think it's important for you to spend some time with your father's side of the family. After he died out here, I swore never to come back. But—"

"Wait," Max interrupted. "Dad's accident happened here? At the place you're taking me?"

His mother nodded.

Max sat back in his seat and gazed forward. It was the only clue she had ever given him about his father's death.

"Mom?" he began.

"Yes, honey?"

"When are you going to tell me what really happened to Dad?"

The question was simple, but it ran deep and wide inside of him, like a story with no ending.

Max had no memories of his father. When other kids' dads visited them at school, he pretended not to care that his own dad could never come. When other kids played catch with their dads at the park or in the yard, he turned his head so that he wouldn't have to feel the pain of missing his own father. And yet, he had never known *why* his dad wasn't there. The only thing he possessed that had once belonged to his father was the faded red hoodie he was wearing now—the hoodie his grandparents had sent to him a few days before on his twelfth birthday.

Max played with the zipper as he watched the shadows of trees creep over his mom's face. She glanced over at him and opened her mouth to speak. Max was sure that he was finally about to get some answers. But her eyes dimmed. Her lips sealed. And her gaze turned forward.

"I've already told you. Your father died in a hunting accident when you were a baby," she said.

But Max sensed there was more she wasn't telling him. And he wanted to know the truth. He wanted to know why his father wasn't there and why he had felt so lonely all his life.

Even so, he regretted asking her the question. He could see the pain in her eyes, and he promised himself he would never ask her again. But what he didn't know was that the answer to his question lay just up ahead, at the end of the slithering road.

2

CABIN IN THE WOODS

The minivan pulled up in front of a log cabin that had been built far back in the woods. Max looked out the window and saw ivy crawling across the shingled roof and up the stone chimney. Several stones and shingles were missing, and the downstairs windows were boarded up. He thought the house looked abandoned. Or even haunted.

This is the kind of place where ax murderers hide dead bodies, he thought.

He put his iPad in his backpack, climbed

out of the van, and followed his mom up the stone pathway to the front door, lingering a few steps behind her. The air smelled like chimney smoke mixed with fresh pine. Red and brown leaves crunched beneath his feet, and a cool breeze tickled his face, reminding him that it was late October.

When he stepped onto the front porch, it creaked, and he thought he might fall straight through the floorboards. Thick cobwebs hung in every corner. The sign above the door read, *Welcome to the Bloodnights'*.

His mom knocked, and he sensed that she was nervous or afraid. She had always been protective of him because he was her only child. But this felt different.

"Let's see—today's Saturday. I'll pick you up on Tuesday, so you'll only miss a couple days of school." She turned to him. "You'll be back just in time for Halloween. Have you decided on a costume yet?"

"Mom, I already told you—I'm getting too old to go trick-or-treating. I'll just help you hand out candy this year and scare the kids that come to the door."

"You're never too old for trick-or-treating," she said.

Then she knocked on the front door again. Harder this time.

"Don't forget—it's very important that you listen to everything your gramps and grammy tell you while you're here. Understand?"

Max nodded, and his mom knocked one last time.

Still, no one answered.

She cupped her hand above her eyes and peered through the nearby window. The inside of the house was dark.

"That's strange. Their letter said to come this afternoon."

"Why don't you just call them?" Max asked.

"Ha!" His mom laughed. "Your gramps and grammy with a phone? That'd be the day. You'll soon learn that things out here are . . . different. Why don't you go check around back and see if anyone's there?"

"But this place gives me the creeps," Max argued, his heart pounding at the thought of going anywhere on the property alone.

"Don't be silly. It's just an old house," his mother said.

Reluctantly, Max walked off the porch and around the corner toward the back of the house. As soon as he was out of his mom's sight, grim visions invaded his thoughts.

He imagined scenes from all the scary movies he had watched by himself late at night when other kids his age were attending birthday parties and sleepovers. Killer clowns and lagoon monsters, possessed dolls and ghost cannibals.

"Don't be silly," he told himself, echoing his mother's words.

He arrived at a screened-in porch. It was so dark that he could barely make out the hoard of clutter resting on the other side of the screen: rusted lanterns, cobwebbed shelves, and framed photographs of family members Max had never seen before.

He knocked on the door.

But no one answered.

He knocked again.

Still, nothing.

Just then, a tall shadow crept over him.

He turned around.

And froze.

There, looming above him, was a stranger.

Holding a bloody ax.

3

FOLLOW THE RULES

"**N**o!" Max shouted, cowering beneath his backpack.

Trembling, he waited for the pain of being cut in half. He had always wondered what murder victims' final moments felt like. And now he was about to find out.

But the pain never came.

"Max, what are you doing?" he heard his mother's voice call out.

Max opened his eyes and saw the ax hanging at the tall stranger's side. The old man wore faded overalls and muddy work boots. The crow's feet in the squints of his eyes told the story of his years, and the smoke from his corncob pipe matched the color of what little hair he had left.

"This is your gramps," Max's mom said.

Max stood on the porch steps, feeling foolish for mistaking his own grandfather for an ax murderer.

"Let me get a good look at you, boy," Gramps said warmly, setting down the ax and holding Max's shoulders square to him. "Just as I thought. You're the spitting image of your father when he was your age. Especially in that red hoodie. He used to wear that thing all the time."

Gramps hugged him, and Max felt the cold metal buttons of the old man's overalls against his cheek.

"And this," Max's mom continued, "is your grammy."

Max watched as an old woman walked up beside his mother, dragging a slaughtered hog by its hoof. She wore a bloodstained apron over a denim dress, and her silver hair was tied up in a bun.

"We've dreamed about this day for so long," Grammy said, and leaned down to kiss Max's cheek. "It will be good to have some young blood around here to help with the chores."

"Chores?" Max asked. His mom shot him a disapproving look. "I mean, thank you for having me."

Grammy heaved the dead hog onto a butcher's slab near the porch, then turned to Max's mom. "Won't you stay for dinner, dear? It's been so long since we had a good chat."

Max's mom hesitated and glanced out at the surrounding woods. She seemed anxious about something.

"Thanks, but I—I'd like to get back to the city before nightfall," she said. She knelt down in front of Max. "I'll pick you up in a few days. Don't forget to listen to your gramps and grammy. Okay?"

She leaned forward and kissed his forehead. Then she whispered something to Grammy that Max had the feeling he wasn't supposed to hear: "Please keep him safe."

Grammy gazed back at her solemnly.

Then Max watched his mom climb back into the minivan and disappear down the winding dirt road, desperately wishing he could go with her.

"Well," Gramps said, patting Max's back. "How 'bout we show you to your room?"

Max nodded, and the three of them walked inside the cabin.

He was surprised to find that it was more spacious than it looked from the outside. The ceilings were high, and everything in the house had an old-fashioned appearance, as if it had been teleported from some other time. There were antique lamps and rocking chairs, moth-eaten couches and cast-iron pots and pans. And the hallways were lined with shelves full of glass jars, each marked with a piece of masking tape labeled with strange herbal names.

But the most unusual thing of all was that

every wall in the cabin was covered with taxidermied animal heads.

Everywhere Max looked, there were stuffed and mounted deer, bobcats, turkeys, mountain lions, and buffalo staring back at him. From the look of it, his father's family were serious hunters.

"Your father used to be the best hunter in Wolf County, you know," Gramps said.

"I thought he was a scientist," Max replied.

"Being a scientist is what made him a good hunter. He could read the signs of nature better than any of us, and he was always coming up with new contraptions and experiments."

Max continued examining the animal heads. "If it's called 'Wolf County,' then why aren't there any wolves on your walls?"

The old man spoke with regret in his voice. "There used to be quite a few wolves in these parts, but they haven't been around in years."

Gramps and Grammy turned the corner and led Max up a creaking staircase. Each step groaned beneath their feet, like creatures waking from an ancient sleep. When they arrived at the top of the stairs, Grammy opened the first door in the hallway.

"This was your father's room," she said. "You and your parents stayed here when you were a baby. It's not much, but it's cozy. Why don't you get settled, then take a look around the farm before supper."

Max glanced around at the wood-planked walls. A strange map or calendar hung on the wall next to the bed, displaying the phases of the moon. Beside the nightstand was an antique telescope looming over a stack of astronomy magazines. It was aimed out the window to a dozen rows of pumpkins speckling out into the distance toward the neighbors' two-story house, which sat on a hill.

And there on the nightstand was a shiny silver dagger. Max couldn't take his eyes off it.

"It was your father's knife," Gramps said. "We keep it there in remembrance. He rarely went anywhere without it."

Max walked over and looked down at it,

thinking of all the times his father's hands had held that same knife.

"Is there a place where I can charge my iPad?" Max asked, looking around for an electrical outlet.

"I'm afraid there ain't a lick of electricity in this house," Gramps replied.

"But . . . how do you do anything without electricity?" Max asked, just now realizing that he hadn't seen a single light bulb in the house. Only lanterns and candles.

"We prefer a simpler life than most," Gramps continued. "Self-reliance is the key to our survival."

At Gramps's words, Grammy cleared her throat. "And you'll survive just fine too. As long as you follow the rules," she said. She sounded far more serious than she had only a moment before.

"What rules?" Max questioned.

If there was anything he despised more than the absence of electricity, it was *rules*. He had never been good at following them at school, at home, or even at the arcade.

"Really, there's just one," Grammy corrected him. "Your father always had a hard time with it, and, well—"

Gramps and Grammy exchanged a knowing look.

Then Gramps leaned forward.

"Listen closely, boy. No matter what you do while you're here, don't cross the barbed-wire fence into the eastern forest."

"Why? What's in the forest?" Max asked.

Gramps's voice grew deeper and more grave.

"Monsters," he whispered.

Max started to laugh, but then saw that Gramps's eyes were dead serious.

He gulped.

"Monsters?" Max said with a shaky voice. He loved monsters in movies and in his games, but the prospect of *real* monsters, well, that was something else.

"Oh, Gramps, you don't have to be so dramatic," Grammy said, swatting the old man's arm. "The boy just got here. No need to overwhelm him with such talk."

But Max could tell there was some truth to what Gramps was saying.

Gramps grunted, perturbed that Grammy had interrupted him. He looked at Max and continued, "You'll be safe as long as you don't go into that forest. And be sure you wear that hoodie zipped up wherever you go. It'll protect you. Especially during the next three nights. Oh, and it's very important that you don't trust anyone while you're here—not even the neighbors."

"How come? What happens during the next three nights?" Max asked.

Gramps put his hand on Max's shoulder.

"The full moon," he warned.

Gramps's eyes—those big, hollowed eyes—seemed plagued with fear. From the look on his and Grammy's faces, Max sensed that his family was petrified of the full moon.

The only question was: *Why?*

4

PUMPKIN SECRETS

Max wandered along the edge of the neighbors' pumpkin patch, wishing he was back home playing his Xbox. He already missed the electric pulse of the city—the noises, the movement, the surprises at every turn. Out here in the middle of nowhere, everything was too still, too quiet, and too boring.

What kind of people don't have electricity in their house? This is the twenty-first century, he sulked. *What am I supposed to do for the next three days?*

He glanced down at his red hoodie. The

silver zipper gleamed in the afternoon light. He wondered how a piece of clothing could protect him from anything other than cold weather.

Max then noticed a disfigured pumpkin growing nearby. It looked like an old, shriveled-up witch with tumors growing out of her face. He was just about to kick it over when a gentle voice invaded his ears. . . .

"Good afternoon, Mrs. Fezzywig! Oh, hello there, Mr. Prickles! How are the kids, Mrs. Wormsworth?"

Max turned and saw a girl about his age wearing overalls, her long brown braids bouncing around like jump ropes as she skipped through the pumpkin patch. She patted each pumpkin, speaking to them as if they were her best friends.

Max couldn't decide whether he should say something, partially in fear of disturbing her daydream, but also because he suspected she might be crazy.

"Uhh—hmm." He cleared his throat, deciding it best to make his presence known.

The girl froze. She looked up at him for an awkward moment with her soft brown eyes.

"Do you have names for all the pumpkins?" Max finally asked, noticing that the blue ribbon in her hair matched the color of the sky.

"Only the orange ones," she teased with a playful smirk.

They both laughed. Max immediately liked her.

"I'm Max Bloodnight," he said, putting out his hand.

"I'm Jade Howler. I live next door," the girl said, pointing to the white, two-story house beyond the pumpkin patch. "You're not from around here, are you?"

"Is it that obvious?" Max asked.

She shot a look at his trendy tennis shoes, the newest Vans on the market. They were a stark contrast to her muddy, well-worn boots.

"Lucky guess," she said with a grin. "As you can imagine, we don't get many city kids around here."

"I'm staying with my gramps and grammy,"

Max said, motioning toward the cabin.

The brightness in Jade's eyes instantly dimmed.

"Oh," she said.

"What's wrong?" he asked.

Jade glanced down at the ground, unsure if she should say anything.

"My dad tells me to stay away from them."

"Really?" Max asked. "I just met them, but they seem nice."

"Probably because you're their grandson," Jade said. "But my dad tells me to stay away from pretty much everyone."

Max considered this for a moment. And then he remembered that Grammy had told him not to trust anyone either—even the neighbors.

"What does your dad do?"

"He's a pumpkin farmer."

Max looked around at the sea of pumpkins, realizing Jade's father had planted every one of them.

"So, what do you do for fun out here besides naming pumpkins?" he asked, hoping to ease his way out of the conversation. "Don't get me wrong. I'm sure you have to make friends however you can in a place where there are only six hundred and thirty-four people in the entire county, but—"

"There used to be more people here," Jade revealed.

"What happened to all of them?" he asked.

Jade took a careful step toward Max.

"They disappeared."

Max felt the breath leave his lungs.

"Disappeared?" he repeated. "I figured they had all just moved away over time."

Jade shook her head and stepped closer to Max.

"I'll tell you what I heard at school, but you can't tell your grandparents that I told you anything, okay? People around here don't really like to talk about it."

"Okay," Max promised, already feeling guilty.

He was torn between his desire to obey his grandparents and the curiosity he now felt about what Jade was saying. He wasn't sure who to trust.

That's when Jade gestured for them to start walking out of the pumpkin patch and through the nearby field . . .

Toward the forest.

5

THE PEOPLE WHO DISAPPEARED

"I heard at school that it all happened twelve years ago," Jade began, looking around to make sure no one was watching. "Chickens, hogs, sheep, and other livestock started going missing from the nearby farms. They vanished in the middle of the night. Always during the full moon."

"The full moon?" Max asked.

"Yeah. Even dogs and cats started disappearing. A few were found at the edge of the forest with their heads missing. But then . . . *people* started vanishing too."

Max felt his stomach churning. He couldn't believe something so savage had occurred in a place as unpopulated as Wolf County.

"Did they catch whoever did it?" he asked.

"You mean *what*ever did it?" Jade corrected him.

Max's eyes widened.

Jade went on, "My friend told me that soon after the disappearances began, people started claiming they saw a wolf pack late at night, led by a giant wolf, walking on its hind legs, wearing human clothes."

"Like a . . . werewolf?" Max asked, imagining the furry Wolfman from his all-time favorite movie, *The Monster Squad*.

Jade nodded.

"There's no such thing as *real* werewolves." Max laughed nervously. "Those kids at school are probably just making up stories."

"Tell that to all the people who saw it," Jade challenged him. "Tell it to the hunters."

"Hunters?"

"Yeah. As soon as the disappearances began,

a hunting party was put together to track down and kill the beast. They ended up killing every last wolf in the forest. There isn't a single one left."

Max felt his heart skip a beat.

So that's why there aren't any wolves around, he thought, starting to put the puzzle pieces together.

"My gramps said that my dad was the best hunter in the county. Maybe he was part of the hunting party. He died in a hunting accident when I was a baby," he revealed. "Out here near the farm. About . . . twelve years ago."

Max's and Jade's eyes met in horrified realization. It struck Max that his father may have been killed while trying to hunt down the beast. It was his first clue—a key to help unlock the mystery that had always haunted him. From the pale look on his face, Jade could tell what he was thinking.

"I'm sorry," she said. "If it makes you feel any better, I miss my mom too."

"Did she die during the disappearances?" Max asked.

"No. She died of cancer when I was seven. It's sort of a . . . different kind of monster."

"I'm—I'm really sorry," Max said.

Just then, they arrived at the edge of the eastern forest. A barbed-wire fence stood between them and the dark woods.

"My grandparents told me not to go in the forest," Max said. "Have you ever gone in?"

"No," Jade replied. "My dad says it's too dangerous. Sometimes, I hear strange sounds coming from it late at night. *Unnatural* sounds."

Max thought of his grandparents' warning and how afraid they had seemed of the forest. As he peered into the woods, he imagined what secrets might be hiding within. And he wondered if there might be more clues about his father. He didn't know why, but something in him—morbid curiosity, perhaps—wanted to step into it. It almost seemed to call to him.

But then he heard something that changed his mind . . .

6

I DON'T EAT MEAT

The man's deep, threatening voice made Max's and Jade's blood curdle. They slowly turned, knowing they had nowhere to hide.

"I said—what are you doing here, Jade?" the stranger asked again, slamming his work shovel into the ground. He was clean-shaven, tall as a doorway, and his overalls straps dripped over his shoulders like denim waterfalls.

Jade stepped toward him defensively. "Dad, we were just walking, and—"

"I've told you to stay away from these woods. They're not safe," her father admonished. "And how many times have I told you not to talk to strangers?"

He peered down at Max suspiciously. The farmer's eyes were the grayest Max had ever seen. Grayer than a storm cloud.

"I'm—I'm sorry, Mr. Howler," Max apologized. "I'm staying next door with my gramps and grammy, and your daughter was just—"

"You're a Bloodnight boy?" he interjected.

Max nodded.

Mr. Howler stared at him.

"All the more reason to stay away from my daughter, then," Mr. Howler warned, jabbing his finger into Max's chest. "You keep on your side of the pumpkin patch, and we won't have any problems. Understand?"

He grabbed Jade's arm and began leading her across the field toward their house.

She glanced back at Max, embarrassed, and mouthed the words *I'm sorry*.

At dinner that evening, Gramps and Grammy sat at the heads of the table, spooning food out of half a dozen bowls and passing them around to Max. He stared down at his plate of juicy meat and couldn't help thinking about how that very meat had been walking around on the farm earlier that morning in the form of a living, breathing hog. It was the first time he had ever seen his food before it was butchered.

"Ain't you gonna eat, boy?" Gramps's gruff voice boomed from the other end of the table.

"I—I don't eat meat," Max confessed, wishing his mom had stayed for dinner to explain his dietary habits.

"Don't eat meat?" Gramps asked.

"I'm a vegetarian," Max said.

Gramps laughed a hearty chuckle, but soon realized that Max wasn't joking. The old man leaned back in his chair and squinted at Max, sizing him up.

"How ya supposed to grow right if you don't eat meat?" Gramps asked.

"I get protein in other ways, like cashews and protein shakes and—" Max stopped when he saw the incredulous look on Gramps's face.

"We have mashed potatoes and green

beans in those bowls beside you," Grammy chimed in, trying to break the tension. "By the way, did you have a nice look around the farm this afternoon?"

Max wanted to ask Gramps and Grammy about everything that Jade had told him—the disappearances twelve years ago, if they had ever seen the man-wolf, and why everyone was so afraid of the eastern forest. But he wasn't sure how to bring it all up.

"I—I met the neighbors," Max said. "The girl next door and I went walking around, and she said that—"

Before Max could finish, Gramps set down his fork and turned to Max.

"Listen to me, Max—you need to stay away from those folks," Gramps chided. "You can't trust anyone around here. It's safer for all of us that way."

"Yes, better stay on this side of the pumpkin patch," Grammy added.

"Why?" Max asked. "Does it have something

to do with the disappearances twelve years ago?"

Gramps and Grammy exchanged a surprised look. They didn't say anything for a long moment. Then Grammy put her palm to her forehead and moaned. "Darn migraines." She took a pill from a prescription bottle in her pocket, put it in her mouth, then glanced out the window toward the horizon.

"It's past sunset," she said. "Gramps, don't forget to lock up the barn after dinner. Just in case. The moon should be coming up any minute now."

Gramps glanced at the rifle case in the corner of the room. He then grunted as he tore a piece of meat with his teeth.

Max thought it was a peculiar exchange but didn't say anything. He assumed that locking the barn before nightfall was a normal chore on the farm.

But something about it felt . . .

Odd.

Like they were hiding something from him. Something secret.

What are they so afraid of during the full moon?

Then he remembered his conversation with his mom earlier that day.

"My mom said that you had some things of my father's that you wanted to pass down to me," he said. "That's why I'm here, isn't it?"

"Well, uh, we're still working on getting it all together," Gramps replied.

"Yes, dear," Grammy added. "We want it to be a surprise."

Later that night, Max lay in bed, watching a moth flutter against the hissing lantern on his nightstand. The cool night air swept through the screen of his open window, rustling the pages of a book resting atop a nearby shelf.

The sounds of the night were unfamiliar to him: crickets, frogs, cicadas, and owls. Back in the city, Max could only hear sirens and horns as he fell asleep every night.

Soon, he heard something stir outside.

He sat up, looked out the window, and saw Gramps locking up the barn. A few moments later, Max heard Gramps come back inside the cabin and start talking to Grammy.

Quietly, Max climbed out of bed and cracked open his door. He saw Gramps and Grammy standing in the den below, their faces aglow with drowsy light from the candle Grammy held in her hands.

He could faintly hear their voices . . .

"His mother said that he doesn't fit in at school," the old woman whispered. "Said he seems lonely."

"His father was the same," Gramps returned.

"Do you think it's too dangerous for him to be here?" Grammy asked. "I mean, he hasn't learned how to protect himself yet."

"Better here with us than anywhere else," Gramps said. "We just have to keep him away from the forest and the neighbors, and everything will go as planned."

Max heard them walk up the stairs toward their bedroom at the end of the hall. He pushed his ear harder against the door, and he heard Grammy's voice once again.

"You really think he's ready to know the truth about what happened to his pa in those woods?" she asked.

"We don't have much of a choice now. The full moon will be at its peak on the third night, and the new beast will arise. We have to make sure that Max is ready to protect himself. The talismans can only help so much," Gramps said, then Max heard their bedroom door click shut.

The new beast will arise? Max repeated in his mind, chilled by the words. *Protect myself? And what talismans?*

A moon-scented breeze seeped through his window screen and rushed over him. He looked out toward the veiled forest.

"What happened to you in those woods, Dad?" he murmured.

Uncomfortable, he unzipped his hoodie

and tossed it onto a nearby chair. "Silly hocus-pocus," he scoffed, skeptical of what Gramps had said about the hoodie somehow being able to protect him. Max then lifted the silver dagger from the nightstand and hid it in the top drawer.

As soon as they go to sleep, I'm going to look around the house for answers, Max thought. *If I can figure out what Grammy and Gramps are talking about, then maybe I can find out what happened to my dad.*

He watched the full moon peeking over the horizon. His mouth stretched into a yawn, and he lay back down in bed and closed his eyes.

Sometime in the night, he awoke to a ghastly howl.

Just outside his window.

7

MISSING

Max woke up covered in sweat. He glanced at the antique clock on the nightstand and saw that it was already three o'clock in the morning.

I feel like I just ran five miles, he thought, peeling the damp pajamas from his skin. *I must have had a nightmare.*

He sat up and looked out the window. An eerie fog drifted over the earth, as if the moon had leaked a ghostly vapor. Just as he was about to lie back down, he noticed a strange light below in the pumpkin patch, jouncing around like an angry firefly.

"A flashlight?" Max whispered, pressing his face against the cold windowpane.

The beam hopped wildly, as if drawing in cursive upon the ground.

At first, Max thought his eyes might be playing tricks on him, but then he saw the silhouette of two long braids.

"Jade?"

Max grabbed the lantern, put on his shoes and his father's hoodie, then walked across the room. He was surprised to find his bedroom door already open and muddy footprints tracked all over the floor.

Where did this mud come from? Did someone come in here while I was asleep?

He stuck his head into the hallway. There was no sign of anyone stirring in the house, so he tiptoed toward the stairs at the end of the hall.

As he passed by Gramps and Grammy's

bedroom, he stopped and peeked inside. The lantern light revealed his grandparents fast asleep in their bed.

When he finally arrived outside, the cool fog swept over him, conjuring goose bumps all over his body. The soft light of the full moon bled through the clouds, making the world feel haunted and dreamlike.

The flashlight beam was closer now. Right next to the barn. Max ran toward it, until he could see Jade's frantic eyes.

"Jade! What are you doing out here so late?" he asked.

In her panicked state, she hardly stopped to acknowledge Max's presence.

"It's Petunia! She's missing!" Jade said.

"Petunia?" Max asked, confused. "Is that one of your pumpkins?"

"No. Petunia is my dog. She always sleeps in my room, but I haven't seen her since dinner," Jade explained.

"Maybe she met another dog, and—" Max began.

"No, no. That's not like Petunia," Jade replied, on the verge of tears. "I have to find her. She sheds when she's scared, so it should be easy to track her once I find her trail."

Max looked out at the nearby field but saw no movement. The night was quiet and still.

"Did you ask your dad if he's seen her?"

"He's on the night shift at the lumber-yard," Jade replied. "Besides, he'd kill me if he knew I was out here in the middle of the night. Especially with you."

Max recalled her father's dreary gray eyes, which had looked so threateningly at him earlier that afternoon. The eyes that had reminded him of a storm cloud.

"I'll help you look for her," Max offered.

Jade relaxed. But just as a thin smile began to form upon her lips, a dog barked in the distance.

It was coming from the forest.

"Did you hear that?" Jade asked, tensing up once again.

Max nodded.

Jade immediately began walking toward the woods. Max followed.

"Petunia!" she shouted. "Petunia! Here, girl!"

Jade stopped at the barbed-wire fence and shined her flashlight along the ground. That's when she and Max both saw . . .

Paw prints. Leading into the forest.

Jade glanced at Max, and he could tell what she was thinking.

"Just for a few minutes, okay?" Jade pleaded. "We'll stay in the shallow part of the forest, then come right back. Petunia couldn't have gone far."

"I don't know," Max said. He was usually up for breaking rules, but in the daytime when it wasn't pitch-dark. "Those don't look like normal paw prints. Maybe we should come back tomorrow. When it's light out. I mean, we don't even have anything to protect ourselves with. What if—"

"Please. I don't want to go alone," Jade admitted.

Max could sense the desperation in her voice. But as he peered into the darkness, everything inside him told him not to enter.

Gramps's warning soon haunted his thoughts. *No matter what you do while you're here, don't cross the barbed-wire fence into the eastern forest.*

Max debated whether to turn back.

There could be anything in there, he thought. And then he remembered a single word Gramps had mentioned that afternoon . . . *monsters.*

"I can't go in there without you." Jade's voice broke his trance.

Max studied the anguish in her eyes and took a deep breath. He looked up at his bedroom window in the distance, wishing he had grabbed his father's dagger out of the nightstand drawer. But he couldn't risk waking up his grandparents now, and there was no time to waste.

Reluctantly, he zipped up his hoodie. And together, he and Jade walked into the forest.

8

INTO THE WOODS

"Petunia! Where are you, girl?" Jade cried out again and again.

The beam of her flashlight sliced through the darkness as she and Max wandered through the misty woods.

Max counted their steps, thinking that if they became lost, they could simply turn around and walk straight back to where they had started.

One, two, three, four . . .

With each step they took, he felt his pulse

rise and his breath quicken. Something about the path felt strangely familiar.

Deeper and deeper into the forest, they traveled.

Over fallen logs.

Across a rickety creek bridge.

And through a tangle of brush.

Until they arrived at a swamp.

It was veiled with moss and dead reeds. The water looked black, like a giant pool of ink. The sounds of the night rattled in Max's ears like a macabre symphony: frogs croaked from the banks, crickets chirped, and owls hooted.

"What is this place?" Max asked.

"I'm not sure," Jade answered. "But it looks scary. I hope Petunia didn't come this far."

Max was just about to recommend that they turn around when he saw something at his feet that made him shudder.

A trail of blood.

Speckled with bits of white fur.

Leading to the other side of a nearby tree.

"Oh!" Jade cried, turning away. It took her a moment before she could speak. "Is—is it Petunia?"

Max crept forward and peered around the trunk of the tree. On the other side were the mauled remains of a small animal that had recently been eaten. Its fur was scattered around like pieces of cotton.

"She should be wearing her silver dog tag. Do you see it?" Jade asked, now crying.

Max had never seen anything so disgusting, but he didn't want to let on how gory the scene actually was. He looked around for the dog tag but found nothing.

"H-honestly, Jade . . . there's not much left to see," Max said.

This only made Jade cry harder.

But then Max saw something peculiar.

Something pink.

The victim's long, furry ears.

"It's—it's not a dog," Max said, morbidly relieved. "It's a rabbit."

Jade opened her eyes, hurried to the other

side of the tree, and knelt down beside the slaughtered creature.

"It's not Petunia!" she declared, feeling both relieved and saddened by the sight of the dead rabbit. "But the blood is fresh, like something just attacked it."

It was then that Max looked out over the marsh and saw the fog dissipating. Beyond it, he noticed something he hadn't seen before.

"What is that?" he asked, rising to his feet.

Jade went pale.

An odd shape loomed before them on the other side of the swamp . . .

. . . shadowy . . .

. . . ominous . . .

Like a monster.

9

HOUSE OF THE BEAST

Max's eyes adjusted, and he saw that the threatening shape was not a monster at all, but a dilapidated old shack.

The stone chimney was half missing, and patches of the roof were covered in vines. And the windows—those grimy, dark windows that might as well have been black mirrors into another dimension—looked straight out of "The Legend of Sleepy Hollow."

Suddenly, a light flicked on inside the shack!

Max and Jade quickly hid behind a cluster of gnarled roots coiling out of the ground.

Max could see the silhouette of someone—or some*thing*—moving inside. The stranger wore a wide-brimmed hat and looked larger than a normal person.

"That must be the hermit of the eastern forest," Jade said, pointing to the window where the man stood.

"The who?"

"My dad said he left Wolf County years ago. He was one of the hunters in the hunting party—the one who killed the beast. I've only heard stories about him, but—"

Just then, Max thought he saw the hermit's silhouette begin to twist and turn. The man's movements grew more violent, and it looked like something was trying to claw its way out of him. Then the light went out, and the shack grew dark again.

"We should get out of here," Max urged.

"But we have to find Petunia," Jade reminded him.

"We're already too far into the forest," Max said. "We can come back tomorrow during the day to look for her. But you and I need to get out of these woods. *Now*."

Jade looked at the shack again.

"The paw prints lead right to it," she said. "I have to at least look inside to see if she's in there."

Max tried to discourage her, but Jade was already running toward it.

He followed after her, trying to keep up. When they arrived at the side of the shack, they pressed their backs up against the outer wall beneath the window of the room where Max had seen the hermit contorting. Jade tried to peek inside one of the windows, but even up close it was too dark to see anything.

"I don't want to turn on my flashlight. It's too bright. Can you hold up your lantern?" she asked.

Max slowly lifted his light to the window, and the two of them stood on their tiptoes, trying to get a better look.

But before their eyes had time to fully adjust, they both froze in fear.

Something stared back at them from the other side of the window.

Something big.

And furry.

With razor-sharp fangs and bloodthirsty eyes.

"W-w-wolf!" they cried out at the same time.

Max fell backward in fright, dropping the lantern.

The glass shattered.

The flame extinguished. All went dark.

"Run!" Jade shouted. "The hermit's a—a—"

"Werewolf!" Max cried out.

The two of them sprinted back into the forest, skeleton-finger branches scratching their faces. Max thought he could feel the beast's breath on the back of his neck and hear it trailing right behind him.

"Faster!" he shouted to Jade.

Back across the bridge.

Over the fallen logs.

Faster.

Panting.

Faster.

But as Max climbed back through the barbed-wire fence, his red hoodie caught on its piranha teeth.

"No, no, no," he cried, trying to free himself.

He glanced back into the woods and thought he could hear the ravenous sounds of the beast drawing nearer.

And nearer.

Was it all in his imagination?

Jade turned back to help Max. She reached for the barbed wire and pushed him out of his hoodie. He tumbled to the ground.

"You run toward your grandparents' cabin, and I'll run to my house," she yelled. "Maybe we can throw off the scent."

"I have to get my father's hoodie before—"

"There's no time!" Jade urged.

"You don't understand! Gramps said it will protect me," Max challenged her, no longer thinking the hoodie a silly precaution.

"A lot of good it's doing you!" Jade called back.

Max didn't say anything.

Jade looked at him for a moment, then finally commanded, "Just go! I'll shine my flashlight from my window to let you know I'm safe!"

Max tore through the ghostly field. Up ahead, he saw the shape of his grandparents' cabin, and wondered if he would make it there alive.

His heartbeat and breath quickened. He sensed that at any moment his legs could be ripped out from beneath him or fangs could tear into his shoulder. But before he knew it, he was back in his bedroom. Safe and sound.

Immediately, he looked out the window toward Jade's house. A thin beam of light waved back and forth through the darkness of her upstairs bedroom like a faint lightsaber.

She's okay! he thought. *We're safe now.*

But as he would soon find out, he would never be safe in Wolf County. And when he looked through the telescope to the barbed-wire fence, his red hoodie was no longer there.

10

OLD ENOUGH TO KNOW

"**M**ornin', boy. Time for work," Gramps said, shaking Max's shoulder.

Max slowly stirred in his bed.

"Work?" he groaned.

Gramps tossed a pair of overalls to him, and the straps slapped his face.

"Meet me at the well in five minutes," the old man said, then disappeared out the door before Max could say a word.

Max sat up in bed, stretched his arms, and yawned. He looked around his room and noticed that the mud on the floor was gone.

Who cleaned it up? he thought.

When he peered out the window to the forest, it seemed to be smiling at him. He couldn't help but wonder if his adventure with Jade the night before had all been a bad dream.

Reluctantly, he put on his clothes and went to meet Gramps outside. The sky was tinged with pink and gold, and the pine needles and grass glistened with morning dew.

"Over here!" Gramps called out.

Max saw Gramps beside the well and slowly approached him. The old man handed a tin pail to Max.

"Sleep all right?" Gramps asked, gripping a rusted lever and showing Max how to pump water into the pail.

"Not really," Max admitted, attempting the task.

"Hmm. Well, I hope you're hungry. Grammy's cookin' up a warm breakfast as we speak," Gramps said.

Max suddenly realized that he wasn't hungry at all. In fact, he hadn't been hungry since dinner the night before. He figured that the sight of the slaughtered hog, as well as the rabbit's carcass, had made him lose his appetite.

Max looked out to the forest, recalling the horrors of his nightmare. It had all seemed so real.

"Gramps?" he began. "Does anyone live in those woods?"

Gramps glared down at Max curiously, as if he was suspicious that the boy knew something he wasn't supposed to know.

"Why do you ask?"

Max shifted his weight on his feet and tried to keep a straight face.

"I mean—why did you and Grammy tell me not to go in there?"

"It ain't our property, that's all," Gramps said. "I always told your father the same thing, but he never listened."

Something about the old man's words seemed hollow. Like an eggshell with no yolk inside.

"My father went in there, didn't he? And

that's why he died?" Max asked, determined to get a straight answer.

Gramps accidentally dropped the pail of water. He glanced down at Max with startled eyes. After a brief moment, he took a deep breath and sighed.

"I suppose you're old enough to know now," Gramps said. "But fair warning—there are going to be some things that are difficult for you to learn while you're here."

"Like what?" Max asked.

Gramps knelt beside Max and lowered his voice.

"All right, then. You said that the girl next door told you about what happened around here twelve years ago?" he asked.

Max nodded.

The old man continued, "When the disappearances began, your father was more bothered by them than just about anyone—mainly because he was worried about you and your mom."

"Did he join the hunting party? The one

that killed the beast?" Max asked.

Gramps looked at him, surprised that he knew about such a thing.

"The so-called beast wouldn't have been killed without your father, that's for sure. Not many people know this, but he saved quite a few lives by what he did."

"My father . . . was a hero?"

Gramps nodded, then added, "But not without a cost."

"What cost?" Max asked.

"His life," Gramps whispered.

Max felt his throat close up. His mind raced with questions. Finally learning the truth of his father's death made his absence seem larger and more painful. But still, he wanted to know more.

A thought soon crossed Max's mind that he had never considered before.

"Where—where is he buried?" he asked.

Gramps looked away. Max could see that there was pain in his eyes. But there was something else there too—something Max couldn't decipher.

"He wasn't buried," Gramps said.

Max squinted questioningly.

Gramps continued, "What I mean is, we never found his body."

11

SHARPSHOOTER

Max stared up at Gramps in shock and confusion. But the old man remained silent.

Just then, Max saw an old rifle leaning up against the side of the well. The wood was weathered, and the silver barrel was tarnished.

"It was your father's rifle," Gramps said, observing Max's curiosity. "Though he spent most of his time with his books, he always found time to go hunting. Could shoot a flea off a dog's back from a hundred yards away. He had a gift. Do you know how to shoot?"

Max shook his head no.

Gramps turned and picked up the rifle. He handled it like it was an extension of his own body.

"You unlatch it here, put the bullet in, relatch, then cock it," Gramps explained while demonstrating each maneuver.

He handed the rifle to Max, then picked up a coffee can from the ground near the barn and set it up on the fence.

"Press the butt against your shoulder here, line up the sight, and pull the trigger when you're ready."

Max's hand shook. His heart pounded in his chest.

"Slow and steady," Gramps said, watching Max's every move.

Carefully, Max aimed at the tin can.

He held his breath. Gulped. And pulled the trigger.

POW!

The can didn't move.

Max blushed with embarrassment.

"It's okay. It was only your first try," Gramps encouraged him. "Tell you what. Maybe we're too close."

Gramps walked a hundred yards down the field next to the barn and set the can on a fallen log. It was so far away it looked like nothing more than a tiny speck glinting in the sunlight.

Maybe my dad could shoot a can from a hundred yards away, but not me, Max thought.

When Gramps arrived back at Max's side, the old man said, "Now, there ain't a scope on this old thing, so you'll have to really focus."

Determined to prove himself, Max lined up the sight at the end of the rifle just like Gramps had demonstrated. He could barely see the can.

"Just let your eyes do the work," Gramps whispered.

In that moment, Max relaxed his eyes, and his vision sharpened. He saw the can lined up with the sight.

He pulled the trigger.

POW!

The can popped off the log and rattled into

the grass. Max could hardly believe it.

"Hmm," Gramps said, somewhat surprised. "Lucky shot, boy. You might be a natural, just like your father. You never know when you might need to protect yourself out here."

Max smiled, feeling proud. It was the first time anyone had ever told him he was like his father.

Just then, the meal bell rang from the front porch of the cabin. Max turned to see Grammy standing there in a red-and-white checkered apron, her hands on her waist.

"Max, would you mind gatherin' some eggs from the coop for me? Breakfast is almost ready," she called over to them.

"Sure, Grammy!" he shouted back.

"You go ahead. I'll refill the water pail. Never keep a lady waiting," Gramps said. "We'll talk more about your father later."

Max left Gramps and headed toward the red barn.

It was a ramshackle structure that looked like it might collapse at any moment. There were holes in the walls, its red paint was faded from sun exposure, and the wood-plank siding was rotted.

Max pushed open the barn doors, and a whiff of manure stung his nostrils.

As he approached the chicken coop in the back of the barn, a feather floated right in front of him, landing on the tip of his nose. He then saw a carnival of feathers dancing all around him.

Strangely, there was no clucking.

And when he looked closer . . .

There were no chickens.

Only feathers.

And blood.

12

THE BOY WHO LIED

A few minutes later, Gramps walked out of the barn, scratching his head. He looked disturbed by what he had seen.

Max and Grammy stood nearby, waiting.

"I told you to lock up the barn last night," Grammy said to Gramps, her tone harsher than usual.

"I did lock it up," Gramps said. "Something must have gotten in."

Max's palms were sweaty, and he could feel his heart pounding all the way down in his fingertips. His adventure into the woods hadn't been a nightmare after all! He knew good and well what had invaded the barn and eaten the chickens. And he knew it was his fault. But he was too afraid to tell Gramps.

Just then, a giant creature appeared around the corner of the barn.

"Ahhh!" Max yelped, jumping backward in fright.

Gramps and Grammy turned and saw the large and furry thing standing there. With black eyes, a long snout, and sharp teeth.

But it wasn't a werewolf.

It was a bloodhound.

And it was limping.

Max noticed the silver dog tag gleaming from its neck.

He held the dog still while he read the inscription on the tag:

My name is Petunia.
If lost, please return to the Howlers at
1985 Wolf County Rd.

"*This* . . . is Petunia?" Max mused aloud, gazing upon the enormous dog. For some reason, he had imagined a dog with a name like Petunia to be much smaller than the colossal creature before him. Gramps knelt beside Max and examined the dog's legs and snout.

"She's all scratched up," he said.

"Maybe it was a raccoon," Max suggested, attempting to coax Gramps away from the truth. "Or maybe—maybe Petunia was the one who ate the chickens."

Gramps grunted in disagreement.

"These marks are too big to be a coon's. That's the mark of a—" Gramps paused. His eyes narrowed, and he turned to Max. "Did you cross into the forest last night, boy?"

Max felt his heart drop into his stomach, split in two, and each half fall down his hollow legs and settle in his feet like weights.

"No," he lied, baffled by how Gramps could know such a thing.

Gramps eyed him suspiciously. Max tried to hide his fear.

"You know what they say?" Grammy interjected, trying to break the tension. "The best way to keep a dog from barking in your front yard is to put him in your backyard."

Neither Max nor Gramps laughed.

Grammy continued, "Gramps, why don't you take the dog next door? And Max, why don't you come help me clean inside for a bit? The cellar needs a good goin' through."

She then leaned in to Gramps and whispered something in his ear that Max sensed he wasn't supposed to hear, "We need to keep a closer eye out tonight. We can't wait much longer."

Gramps nodded.

Grammy held out her wrinkly hand to Max, and he took it into his own. He walked beside her back to the house, stepping upon each stone of the leaf-covered pathway.

Before Max walked inside the cabin, he glanced over his shoulder at Gramps. The old man was standing near the barn, staring back at him, a secret locked in his eyes.

13

CELLAR SECRETS

The cellar was cold and dim, like a mortuary. Max swept the floor with an old, crooked broom, making his way through a maze of dusty furniture—a broken bookshelf, an abandoned wardrobe, and a metal gun case. The walls were rotted and covered in cobwebs, and the air smelled musty, like a box of old clothes that hadn't been opened in years.

I should have told Gramps the truth, he thought, wrestling with guilt. *I guess it won't matter anymore once I'm back in the city in a couple of days.*

Max suddenly stopped. A beam of dusty sunlight illumined an old wooden chest resting in the corner of the cellar. The wood was warped, and the top was covered with a layer of dust an inch thick. Its lock was rusted beyond use. And above it was a grimy silver emblem.

He walked closer to get a better look.

The shape of it was unmistakable.

"Wolf?" Max whispered, making out the form of a hungry beast baring its fangs.

Max carefully unlatched the lock and opened the coffer. A moldy scent rose out of it.

Inside was a collection of peculiar relics left over from a childhood long ago: a tin can of baseball cards, G.I. Joe action figures, and a Super Soaker water gun. Mixed in with these forgotten treasures were artifacts from a more grown-up time in life: a framed photograph turned facedown, a worn leather journal, a star-gazing atlas, a camouflaged net, a black pouch used for storing bullets, and a set of hunting magazines.

"What is all this stuff?" Max asked, running

his finger over each item.

He turned over the photograph and gasped. It was as if he had seen a ghost.

In the picture was his mother, at least a decade younger. She was holding Max when he was a baby and standing next to a tall, kind-faced man who had his arms around both of them.

"Dad?" Max said in shock and awe.

He stared at his father's face while gently touching the glass in the frame. He had only seen a few pictures of his father before—it was too hard for his mom to keep photographs of him up in their house.

Gramps was right, he thought. *I do look like my dad.*

After a long moment, Max set down the picture, picked up the leather journal, and opened it. The writing on the first page read:

The Diary of Jedidiah Bloodnight

It was his father's handwriting. Max recognized it from old letters he had once found in his mom's closet.

All of this stuff must have been my dad's, Max thought. *Maybe this is what Gramps and Grammy wanted to pass down to me. Maybe this is why they invited me here.*

He considered closing the chest, so as not to ruin Gramps and Grammy's surprise. But he wanted answers, and he didn't want to wait any longer for the truth. He continued flipping through the pages of the diary, and stopped on the very last entry:

October 31
The wolves are nearly all dead. Time is running out.
I must protect my family at all costs and find a way to complete my experiment.

If I am unsuccessful tonight, then a new beast will surely arise in twelve years.

"So it's true, then?" Max whispered. "My father was hunting the beast. And he died trying to protect us—his family."

He looked up from the diary and noticed a giant drape covering up something behind the chest. He gently lifted the covering, and his eyes grew wide. Beneath it was a table ornamented with glass beakers, coiling funnels, and test tubes. An open chemistry book sat in the middle of it all, filled with indecipherable equations. Taped to the wall behind the table were blueprints of the red hoodie with a silver zipper, the silver dagger, and a glass vial labeled "Liquid Silver."

What was my father doing with a chemistry lab down here in Gramps and Grammy's basement? he wondered. *What was he trying to create?*

He glanced back down at the diary and saw something else written in bigger letters and underlined at the bottom of the last page:

PS I'm leaving behind three talismans in case something happens to me.
The Liquid Silver is the most powerful of them all.
The hoodie and dagger will only hold off the beast for the first two nights of the full moon.
Only by infecting its blood on the third night can it be destroyed forever.

Max looked up from the diary to the sketches on the wall. He examined the drawings of the silver zipper on the hoodie, the silver dagger, and the vial of glowing Liquid Silver. He had encountered all three of the talismans except for the last one. He looked around for it but didn't find anything.

Why is the Liquid Silver the most powerful talisman of all? he wondered.

Just then, something crashed against the cellar window behind him . . .

14

MEET ME AT MIDNIGHT

A shadow moved across the cellar window that connected to the side yard. Someone was standing outside, pounding on the pane.

Max walked across the basement and lifted the window.

"I've been looking all over for you," Jade said, her blue-ribboned braids falling over the window frame like two ropes leading up the side of a castle wall.

"How did you know I was down here?" Max asked.

"Your gramps said that you were doing

some cleaning in the basement, so I snuck over," she replied. "He just brought Petunia by. She's resting back at the house."

"I told you that she'd be okay," Max said.

"Yeah, but did you see those claw marks? Whatever did that to her had to be the creature that chased us through the woods last night. I told my dad everything, but he just got really angry that I had gone into the forest. He said it was impossible that the hermit could be back, and to stay away from the woods."

Max was glad that he hadn't told Gramps and Grammy anything.

"The chickens were all missing from the barn this morning," Max revealed. "Something ate them. Just like you said happened twelve years ago."

Jade gulped, then gazed into the shadows of the basement.

"What if the beast from twelve years ago never really died?" she said.

Max remembered Gramps and Grammy's conversation the night before about a new beast rising during the full moon. His father had written about it in his diary too.

"What made people think the werewolf was dead?" Max asked. "Did anyone actually see it after it was killed?"

"I don't know. That's just what my dad told me," Jade replied. "I did hear Molly White say once at recess that the beast could have been one of our own. And that there might be others."

Max considered this for a moment.

So that's why no one trusts each other in Wolf County—even neighbors, he realized.

It was all too incredible to be believed. Like an episode of *Stranger Things*.

"Listen, I've been gathering clues, and I found one down here, I think. Before my dad died, he was conducting some kind of experiment with silver. I think he was trying to find ways to kill the beast. And the red hoodie I lost last night was a part of it. I have to go back to find it."

"Are you crazy? We almost died in there last night!" Jade reminded him.

"It's the only thing I have that belonged to him," Max said. "And I have to know what happened to my dad out there. There are still too many unanswered questions."

Jade stared at him incredulously. Max was braver than she'd thought. And more insane.

"But, Max, the hermit who lives in that shack *is* the beast," Jade reminded him. "I mean, we saw him transform in the window right before our eyes."

"There are still two more nights of the full moon. Think of all the lives we'll save if we can find a way to stop the beast this time," Max said.

Jade was silent.

"Meet me at the fence at midnight. Okay?" Max added.

"My dad will kill me if he finds out," Jade said.

"He doesn't have to know," Max coaxed her with a mischievous smirk. "Besides, I risked my life to help you look for Petunia last night. You owe me."

Jade thought about it for a long moment.

"Fine," she said. "But you better bring a rifle. *And* some silver bullets."

"Huh?"

"Silver bullets are the only way to kill a werewolf, city boy. You have to pierce its heart. Don't you watch scary movies?" she teased, then disappeared out of Max's view before he could say anything else.

Max knew good and well that silver was the only way to kill a werewolf in comic books and movies, but this was real life. And in real life, there were no such things as monsters. Right? At least that's what he kept trying to tell himself.

Hesitantly, he went back to the trunk and reached for the black pouch used for storing bullets, sensing what might lie inside of it.

But when he looked in the pouch . . .

It was empty.

15

TRAPPED

At dinner that evening, Gramps and Grammy were quiet. Gramps kept looking out the window, as if he was expecting someone.

"Did you get the cellar cleaned up?" Grammy asked.

Max nodded as he chewed a mouthful of green beans.

"Find anything interesting?" Gramps added. "I'm sure there are lots of treasures down there."

"Not really," Max said, wanting to keep his

findings to himself. Every time he had tried to ask Gramps or Grammy about his father, they had only given him vague answers.

Grammy smiled and passed a bowl of mashed potatoes around the table. "Well, it's nice to have you here, Max. This house has felt empty for some time."

"Ever since your pa died," Gramps added solemnly. "We wrote to your mom many times through the years asking her to bring you here, but I think she was afraid of—"

Grammy kicked Gramps's shin beneath the table. Max's eyebrows rose in intrigue.

Afraid of what? he wondered.

Gramps cleared his throat and continued, "Now that you're here, we can right some of our wrongs."

"Oh, don't be so hard on yourself," Grammy said to Gramps, then turned to Max. "Gramps has always blamed himself for your father's death. But it wasn't his fault."

Max wanted Gramps and Grammy to tell

him more, but neither of them said another word the rest of dinner.

Later that night, Max lay in bed watching the clock tick, tick, tick . . .

Toward midnight.

A few minutes before he was supposed to meet Jade at the barbed-wire fence, he crawled out of bed already fully dressed. His plan was to go downstairs, take Gramps's rifle, and sneak out the back door. But he knew if he woke anyone up, his plan would be ruined.

Quietly, he crept toward his bedroom door, put his hand on the cold brass handle, and turned it.

But . . .

It was locked.

From the *outside*.

He tried again.

But it wouldn't budge.

He jiggled it harder, but still nothing.

Gramps and Grammy locked me in! Are they trying to keep me in or keep something out?

Max pounded his fist against the door, then glanced at the clock. Midnight was quickly approaching.

If I don't meet Jade on time, she might chicken out, he worried. *And I won't be able to find the hoodie!*

He rushed to the window and tried to open it. But it was stuck too. He then saw two large nails wedged into the side panels of the frame, blocking the window from being pushed up.

Gramps must have nailed these shut while I was cleaning in the cellar today, Max thought.

He panicked, looking everywhere for a hammer or something helpful to pry the nails. He searched under the bed, in every drawer of the wardrobe, and even in the closet. But there was nothing.

Feeling the weight of defeat, Max sat down on the edge of the bed and stared at the wall. His eyes perused the poster of the moon cycles. Each illustration showed a different moon phase, including the three nights of the full moon. He hadn't noticed it before, but the third night of the full moon was circled multiple times with a red marker. It reminded him of his father's diary entry.

The silver dagger! Max remembered. *It's one of the talismans!*

Knowing he didn't have much time, he rushed to open the nightstand drawer, grabbed his father's knife, and hurried to the window. When he pulled the knife from its sheath, he accidentally touched the silver blade and an odd feeling rushed over him.

What sort of experiment was my dad doing with this thing?

He held the dagger by the leather handle and used the blade as a lever to pry up the nails. It took longer than if he'd had a hammer, but he was eventually able to jimmy the window enough to open it and slip through.

He clumsily climbed across the roof, taking light steps so that he wouldn't wake up his grandparents.

Gramps's rifle! Max remembered. *If I try to go back inside to get it now, I'll wake up him and*

Grammy. This knife will have to do.

Once at the edge of the roof, Max jumped onto a hay bale resting below and tumbled onto his feet. Just as he was about to run to meet Jade . . .

A desperate cry arose from the direction of the forest.

16

MAX MEETS THE BEAST

When Max arrived at the barbed-wire fence, Jade wasn't there.

I'm too late, he thought. *She must have already gone home.*

He gazed into the woods. They were dark and quiet, like something that had been asleep for a thousand years and had no need to make its presence known. He sensed they were hiding something.

Then he saw something that turned his blood cold . . .

A blue ribbon.

Caught on a branch.

Just a few feet on the other side of the barbed-wire fence.

"No," he gasped.

Without a second thought, Max climbed through the barbed wires, grabbed Jade's ribbon, and sprinted into the forest. He squinted, trying to see in the dark, but the canopy of trees above blocked the moonlight.

I have to find her, he thought, his guts a trembling pile of mush.

He searched for hours, looking everywhere. He passed by streams and across narrow ravines. Near caves and burrows. But there was no sign of her anywhere—no sounds, no footprints, no bouncing beam of her flashlight. And no hoodie either.

I hope the hermit—the beast—didn't get her, he thought as he walked by a tree he had already passed a dozen times. He sensed the night was nearly over.

Just as he was about to turn around, a high-pitched yelp blared from behind a nearby bush.

"Jade!" Max whispered in fright.

The cry came again. And again. It was excruciating—like she was wounded or trying to escape!

He hurried as fast as he could toward her, hoping he could get there in time. Branches scratched his arms and legs, and cobwebs stuck to his face as he navigated through the warren of trees.

Soon, Jade's cries turned to whimpers. Max could hear the panic in her voice. It was the sound of a creature that knew it was about to die.

But the closer he came to it, the less it sounded like Jade.

That's—that's an animal, he discerned.

Right then, Max heard another sound. Deep, vicious growling. It rumbled like the engine of an old truck.

Quickly, he hid behind a thicket of brush. He peeked through the mesh of limbs, and saw . . .

The beast!

Faint moonlight poured through an opening in the forest ceiling and illumined the spot where the werewolf stood. Its shoulders were as broad as a tractor. Its snout was as long as a ruler. Its ears were giant pyramids that reached up toward the treetops. And its fur—oh, that terrible, prickly fur—reminded Max more of a porcupine than a puppy. But most striking of all were its razor-sharp fangs, dripping with saliva as it used its giant paws to lift a baby deer toward its gullet!

The deer whimpered helplessly.

I can't just let it die, Max thought, his heart chugging in his chest like a runaway train. *If Jade were here, she'd do something.*

He reached down and felt the ground for a rock. Once he found one with jagged edges, he stood and hurled it with all his might.

It bounced off the werewolf's head, startling the beast.

Max picked up another rock and threw it.

And another.

Until the werewolf dropped the baby deer, and the scared creature ran off into the woods. To safety.

Furious, the werewolf sniffed the air, searching for the scent of its attacker. Max suspected the beast had night vision and could see in the dark. Unsure what to do, Max remained hidden behind the thicket, trying to hold his breath.

Sniff!

Sniff!!

Sniff!!!

The beast's sniffs sounded like a bull about to charge. Max could hear its paws crunching over the fallen leaves on the other side of the tree. Tracking Max's scent. Ready to pounce.

Just as the beast arrived at the thicket, Max hurried and hid behind another tree. The beast sniffed the ground where Max had been standing, and Max knew he didn't have much time. There were no other trees close enough to hide behind without the beast seeing him.

With a shaky hand, Max lifted the silver knife from its sheath. He knew he'd only have one chance to pierce the werewolf's heart.

The beast growled, sensing Max was close by.

It moved quicker.

Louder.

Nearer.

And just as its monstrous eyes peeked around the tree, Max slashed the blade toward it, stabbing with all his might.

The werewolf let out a terrible cry. "Arrooohhh!"

Did I kill it? Max wondered. *Did I stab its heart?*

Max stepped out from behind the tree to survey the wounded creature. But a chill crept over him like a blanket of ice.

I—I missed! Max lamented.

The knife had not pierced the werewolf's heart, but now stuck out of its eye socket like an extension of a gross Halloween mask. Max panicked as he watched the beast yelping in pain as it tried to remove the dagger from its eye.

Suddenly . . .

The werewolf's ears began to transform into human ears, and its paws into human hands.

The silver must repel the beast's nature and turn it back into its human form! Max thought in terror and excitement. *Maybe that's what my father's experiment was all about!*

The werewolf turned and looked right at Max. It growled threateningly.

Max froze, preparing for the beast's revenge. He wanted to see the face of the hermit, the man who had killed his father.

But before its human identity was revealed, it turned and darted off into the woods.

Max wondered if he should track the beast and finish what his dad had started, but he suspected it was no use without the silver dagger.

He felt his arms and legs to make sure he was still all in one piece and was surprised to find that there was not a scratch or a bite mark anywhere on his body.

Soon, his thoughts turned back to Jade.

I hope she escaped before the werewolf could get to her.

Knowing he was also out of time to go look

for the hoodie, he looked toward the horizon. It was just starting to turn a light blue color. Morning twilight.

The sun will be rising soon, he thought. *I need to get back to the cabin before Gramps and Grammy know that I'm gone.*

But it was already too late for that.

17

TELLING THE TRUTH

When Max arrived back at the cabin, the sky was just beginning to lighten.

Gramps was pacing back and forth on the porch with his rifle, shaking his head and mumbling to himself.

At the sight of Max, the old man's eyes widened.

"Max!" he shouted. "Where have you been? We've been looking all over for you!"

Max hurried toward him, and Gramps met him in the yard and hugged him tight.

"I stabbed the werewolf!" Max declared,

trying to catch his breath. "The hermit in the forest—he's the beast!"

"The forest?" Gramps asked, aghast.

Max nodded, deciding to be honest this time.

"How many times do I have to tell you to stay out of those woods?" Gramps shouted. "You've put us all in danger. Do you want to make the same mistakes as your father?"

Max froze, unable to speak.

The old man glared down at him.

"Boy, you can't realize what you've done. We locked you in your room last night to protect you from such dangers. After the incident with the chickens, we couldn't risk another thing like that happening. Like I said, if your scent ever got into the forest—especially during the full moon—it'd be a danger for us all."

Max looked down at the ground, heavy with guilt.

Gramps sighed.

"What's done is done," the old man finally said. "Tonight's the last night of the full moon.

And the important thing is that you're here now. What were you doing in the forest anyway?"

"I was trying to find Jade and my hood—"

"The girl next door?"

"Yes. Have you seen her?"

Gramps hesitated. "As a matter of fact, I saw her and her father getting into their truck not ten minutes ago. Said they were going on a last-minute vacation. They seemed in quite a hurry."

Vacation? Max thought, wondering why they would leave on such short notice.

"But she never said anything to me about it," Max said.

Gramps shrugged.

"I told you not to trust anyone around here."

He then led Max toward the porch steps and opened the front door for him.

"Why don't you go on upstairs and get some sleep? I'm sure you're tired. I'll make us some breakfast when you wake up," Gramps said.

"Where's Grammy?" Max asked.

"She's not feeling well," Gramps explained.

"One of her migraines again. She's going to need some bed rest today, but she'll be back to normal in no time."

Max realized just how tired he was. He dragged himself upstairs to take a nap and stopped to peek inside his grandparents' bedroom.

The lights were off, and the room was pitch-dark. Grammy was lying in bed with her back to the door. Max could hear her softly moaning, so he closed the door so that he wouldn't disturb her.

Poor Grammy, he thought. *I wish I could help her feel better.*

Just then, Max heard Gramps's voice call to him from downstairs. Max peeked over the rails of the second-floor walkway and saw the old man standing below . . .

"I almost forgot!" Gramps said. "I know things have been a bit strange around here, but Grammy and I should have your surprise ready for you tonight. We've been looking forward to it for a while, so no more sneaking away, okay?"

Max nodded, feeling guilty again for having already looked inside the wooden chest.

He watched as Gramps's shadow crawled across the den floor and disappeared into the next room.

Exhausted, Max ambled toward his bedroom and plopped down on his bed.

As soon as his head hit the pillow, he began to think about everything he had experienced since arriving on the farm.

The hermit's transformation.

The bloody chicken coop.

The werewolf he had stabbed.

Somehow, he sensed they were all connected to his father's death. And as he slipped away into a dark, dreamless sleep, he remembered again that the coming night was the final night of the full moon.

When the new beast would arise.

18

HOME INVASION

After Max's nap, Gramps made a big breakfast: bacon for himself, and eggs and chocolate-chip pancakes for Max.

The two of them worked in the garden for the rest of the day, pulling up weeds, pruning the vegetables, and getting ready for harvest. All the while, Grammy rested inside the house.

As Max worked, he thought about the werewolf he had stabbed. He wondered if it was lying dead somewhere in the woods, or if it had made it back to its shack. And then his thoughts turned to Jade and her father. He couldn't figure out why they had left in such a hurry. Had they really decided to go on a last-minute vacation? Or had the hermit frightened them?

That evening, just after sunset, Max sat down on the porch with a warm mug of pumpkin cider. He glanced over his shoulder to make sure no one was watching, then he lifted his father's diary from the front pocket of his shirt. He wanted to know everything that his father knew about the beast and if there were any more clues about his experiment. Max hoped that Gramps and Grammy wouldn't notice that the diary was missing from the chest.

Just as he was about to open to the first page, he looked across the pumpkin patch at the Howlers' house and saw a buttery light glowing in one of their downstairs windows.

Maybe they came back early, he thought.

Just then, he heard Gramps's voice call to him from inside the cabin.

"It's gettin' dark, boy! Ten more minutes, then you better come inside," the old man said. "It's almost time for your surprise."

Max reasoned that if he went back inside the house with Gramps, he might be locked up in his bedroom again for the night. But he needed to talk to Jade—and he knew this might be his only chance.

He put the diary back in the front pocket of his shirt and snuck off the porch.

A moment later, Max was rushing through the pumpkin patch, the autumn air licking his face and the scent of fallen leaves and pumpkin dust fuming into his nostrils.

When he arrived on the Howlers' front porch, he saw that the light was coming from the living room. But it didn't look like anyone was home, and Max wondered if the light had accidentally been left on.

Curious, he knocked on the door.

No one came.

He knocked again.

Still, no answer.

He decided to try the doorknob . . .

When he turned it, to his great surprise, the door creaked open.

The possibility of entering a house without being invited felt illegal.

He stepped inside anyway and looked around.

The air was warm, and he heard the heater wheezing in the nearby hallway. There, he saw dozens of framed photographs hanging on the wall, including a few of Jade's mother holding her when she was a baby. Then he saw that there were lights on in not just one but several rooms.

Maybe the Howlers forgot to turn them off before they left this morning, Max supposed.

But as he searched through the house, he found more peculiar things . . .

The pillows on the couch were all out of place. A cup of cold coffee sat on a wooden lampstand next to an open book. And an antique lamp was shattered on the ground next to an overturned chair, as if there had been a struggle of some kind.

Strangest of all . . .

Two plates sat on the dinner table. And they

were both full of food.

A fork was stuck into a pile of mashed potatoes, which had hardened like toasted meringue. And the water glasses were still full.

It was almost as if the Howlers had left for their vacation right in the middle of a meal. Either that, or they had simply vanished into thin air.

Maybe they heard the werewolf howling last night and decided to leave right away, Max thought, searching for a logical explanation.

Max then heard an odd sound coming from the nearby closet in the entryway.

Scratching. Desperate, spine-tingling scratching.

It sounded like someone trapped in a coffin trying to claw their way out.

He walked toward the sound.

The scraping was coming from *inside* the closet.

Was it Jade? Her father? Or perhaps . . .

Max held his breath.

Then he reached for the handle and turned it.

19

NO TURNING BACK

A creature was in the closet!

A furry, black-eyed, long-tailed creature!
Not just any creature, but a—

Mouse?

The tiny rodent scurried out of the unlit closet and ran right over Max's shoe, causing him to jump in fright. It moved so fast that Max didn't see where it went.

He couldn't help but feel silly for being so afraid of a mouse scratching on the closet door. But then he noticed something unexplainable.

The closet was full of . . .

Suitcases.

They were all zipped up and stacked against one another like books on a bookshelf. A layer of dust blanketed the tops of them, as if they hadn't been used in months or even years.

Who goes on vacation without their suitcases? Max thought, wondering why Mr. Howler and Jade would lie to Gramps. Or . . . why Gramps would lie to Max.

He glanced over at the lamp on the ground and then to the table of food. He began to put the puzzle pieces together just as he saw the full moon beginning to rise outside the window.

That's when he saw . . .

Muddy paw prints.

Leading out the back door.

The hermit, Max thought. *He probably took the Howlers back to his shack, and he's going to eat them beneath the full moon tonight. If they're still alive, there probably isn't much time!*

Max ran into the kitchen, took a knife from the butcher block, and hurried out of the house.

He thought about going to get Gramps, but

he knew the old man would just lock him up again. And he couldn't risk Gramps ruining his plan. So Max dashed across the field.

Under the barbed-wire fence.

And into the woods for the last time.

Twilight dissolved, and darkness fell upon the earth like a plague. Max could feel the eyes of wild creatures watching him from every pocket of the woods. It made him feel vulnerable—like a sheep being led to slaughter.

When he arrived at the hermit's shack, he waited to see if there was any sign of movement inside. But there was no light. No shadows. The entire shanty seemed to be in slumber.

Conjuring up his courage, Max approached the rotting structure.

One step, two steps, three . . .

An owl hooted nearby in warning.

Max stepped onto the porch, and the old wood groaned beneath his feet.

There's no turning back now, he told himself.

Max reached for the door and opened it. The smell of death rushed over him.

The inside of the shack was dark, and Max couldn't see anything. He felt along the walls with his hands until he stumbled upon a wooden dresser with a railroad lantern sitting atop it. He patted the top of the dresser, then frantically searched through the drawers, hoping to find a box of matches.

The top drawer . . .

The middle drawer . . .

The bottom drawer . . .

Finally, he found what he was looking for and quickly lit the wick.

As soon as the light bloomed, Max saw an old rifle hanging on the wall above the dresser, covered in cobwebs. Beneath it, on top of the dresser, was a peculiar leather-bound book. The tome was large and dusty and full of yellowed pages. It looked homemade, like a scrapbook of some kind.

He felt the cover.

It was wrapped in . . .

"Skin?" Max whispered in horror.

Chills ran up his spine and robbed him of breath. He couldn't move—his entire body was paralyzed.

But then he looked closer. The book had splotches of fur all over it. That's when he realized that it wasn't covered with human skin but . . . wolf skin.

Max carefully opened the cover, fearing it might crumble in his hands. Inside was a collection of newspaper clippings and photographs. They were all glued to the curling, tawny pages.

In each picture was the same bearded man wearing a wide-brimmed hat.

"The hermit," Max whispered, remembering seeing him wearing that same hat two nights before when he had transformed into the beast.

And yet, in every single photograph, the hermit was standing over the corpses of . . .

Wolves.

If the hermit is a werewolf, then why would he

want to kill the wolves of the eastern forest? Max wondered.

For the life of him, Max couldn't figure out the riddle.

Then he saw an article that perplexed him even more. The headline was dated twelve years before, and it read:

THE WOLVES ARE DEAD! KILLED BY LOCAL HUNTERS!

In the picture, a group of men was standing over the corpses of several wolves. The hermit was in front of them all, with his foot resting atop the dead body of a giant wolf.

A man-wolf.

The beast!

Max blinked in astonishment.

But Gramps said that my father was the one who killed the beast, he thought, running his fingers over the picture of the hermit. *This man isn't my father!*

As he turned around to explore more of the

shack, the lantern light licked across the room, illuminating the most nightmarish thing that Max had ever seen.

He was being watched.

Not by one . . .

Or even by two . . .

But by a dozen beasts!

20

ONCE AND FOR ALL

The wolves stared back at him, baring their fangs and piercing him with their cold black eyes.

Max's heart raced. Blood pulsed through his veins like hot oil. He couldn't breathe—it felt like someone was sitting on his chest, trying to crush him.

He waited for the beasts to pounce, to rip apart his flesh and devour him. But their furry snouts remained still. Frozen. Lifeless.

That's when Max saw that the wolves were all stuffed. Hunting trophies. Decorations for the hermit's shack.

And they were just wolves—plain old four-legged wolves.

Except for one.

The giant man-wolf nearest to the window stood on only two legs, forever peering out into the dark forest. As if waiting for someone.

And the creepiest thing about it was . . .

It was wearing Max's hoodie.

That's the werewolf I saw in the window two nights ago, Max surmised. *I thought the hermit had transformed, but it was just this stuffed wolf. But why is it wearing my hoodie?*

He stepped closer to get a better look.

Max felt a morbid satisfaction at seeing his father's killer. But another thought soon crept into his mind . . .

Maybe the hermit was bitten by this original beast twelve years ago just before he killed it, and the wolf blood is just now ripening in him.

Just when Max thought he couldn't become any more confused, he saw something that changed every clue, suspicion, and logical thought he had entertained about the hermit.

He glanced down at the scrapbook in his hands and squinted to get a better look at the photograph. That's when he recognized something he hadn't seen before.

The hermit's eyes.

They were as gray as a storm cloud.

Just like . . .

Jade's father! Max thought, overcome with puzzlement. *I almost didn't recognize him with the beard!*

Max remembered what Jade had told him— that her father had always warned her never to go into the forest. But if the reason he forbade his daughter to go into the forest and scared her with tales of a hermit was so that she wouldn't discover his secret obsession, then what was Gramps and Grammy's reason for forbidding Max? Did they already know that the hermit was the beast, and that the beast was Mr. Howler?

Right then, a terrible howl tore through the night. It rattled Max's ears and electrified his brain. It was more excruciating than nails scratching across a chalkboard. Strangely, he felt drawn to it.

He removed the hoodie from the stuffed man-wolf and quickly put it on. The feeling of it wrapped around him made him feel less afraid. He grabbed the rifle from the wall. It had scratch marks on the handle, and the barrel was rusted, as if it hadn't been used in some time.

Max then observed four tiny sluglike stones sitting on the corner of the dresser.

"Silver bullets!" he said in astonishment.

Without time to think, he swiped them into his hand. They felt cold as ice cubes against his sweaty palm. He inserted one of them into the chamber of the gun, just like Gramps had shown him the day before, and put the rest in his pocket.

Then he gathered up his courage.

Hurried to the door.

And headed into the night.

To end the beast once and for all.

21

NOT AFRAID ANYMORE

Max rushed through the maze of trees, his thoughts focused on killing the beast and finding out the truth about his father.

As he traveled through the croaking woods, the night wrapped around him like a blanket. Sucking him in. Devouring him with fear.

He panted for breath as the full moon crawled up its invisible ladder into the sky, spilling its soft glow upon the forest below. All the while, the sounds of the night pounded in Max's ears, as if the volume of the world had somehow been turned up. The crickets, the frogs, and the owls all felt like they were *inside* his head!

Max aimed the barrel of the rifle ahead. He knew that if the beast were to jump out and attack him, he would only have one shot. And he wanted it to count.

Suddenly, a bone-chilling howl sounded in the near distance, causing the hairs on Max's arms to stand up.

"AA-RRR-OOOOO!"

A moment later, a second howl sounded in the distance.

Was it an echo?

Or . . .

Another werewolf?

What if Jade is a werewolf too? Max thought.

He raced toward the howls, knowing the full moon was nearing its peak.

Across the creek bridge.

Over fallen logs.

And then Max saw a beast leap high over the barbed-wire fence and into the field. The werewolf's silhouette ran toward the pumpkin patch. Toward Jade's house.

Panting.

Salivating.

Hunting.

Max tried to catch up, but it was no use. Mr. Howler was much faster. Though, somehow, Max was now running more rapidly than he ever had in his life.

Just when he thought the beast was about to arrive at the Howlers' house, it changed its course.

"No!" Max cried out, watching the werewolf move in the direction of his grandparents' cabin. "I have to warn them!"

Max gripped the rifle tighter in his hands.

He imagined Gramps sitting in the den while Grammy rested in bed. They would never see the beast coming!

Max was still halfway across the field when he saw the werewolf slow down.

Was he injured? Afraid? Preparing to attack?

Max watched as the beast stepped out of

the moonlight and onto the shadowy porch of the cabin.

I have to get closer! This may be my only chance to take a clear shot! Max told himself.

But then something unexpected happened.

As the werewolf crossed the porch . . .

Its fur began to disappear.

Its ears changed shape.

And its snout transformed into a nose.

That's when Max realized . . . the beast wasn't Mr. Howler.

22

THE PATCH

"It can't be!" Max whispered, stopping dead in his tracks.

The air vanished from his lungs.

His knees wobbled.

His blood turned cold.

It was Gramps standing there on the porch, wiping his boots on the doormat and reaching for the door.

Gramps is a werewolf! Max realized in terrified disbelief.

The old man glanced over his shoulder and looked right where Max was standing. Max crouched down in the grass, hoping Gramps hadn't seen him.

After a moment, the old man disappeared inside the house.

Max remained hidden, completely in shock and unsure what to do next.

He looked down at the rifle. He knew that as long as the silver bullet was in the chamber, he could protect himself.

I can't shoot my own grandfather—even if he is a werewolf, he decided. *He wouldn't try to hurt me, would he?*

Max considered running as fast as he could to the nearest town to find help, but something in him wanted to stay. Even if it meant risking his life.

He wanted answers. All of them.

Cautiously, he stood and approached the cabin.

A slight breeze swept over him, making him feel as if he had just passed through a ghost.

He could now see Gramps through the side window of the house, walking from room to room. The old man seemed in a hurry.

Maybe he's coming after me, Max thought, then considered something that didn't make any sense. *But if Gramps was the werewolf I stabbed last night, then why isn't his eye wounded?*

Just as Max remembered the second howl he had heard in the forest, footsteps rustled behind him. Sly, methodical footsteps—like a predator sneaking up on its prey.

He slowly turned . . .

There, looming above him, was someone he never expected to see.

"Going somewhere, dear?" Grammy asked with a mysterious smile stretched across her face.

Max stumbled backward and fumbled the rifle in his hands. He was so terrified that he dropped it.

"I was—I was just—" Max tried to come up with an explanation, but he somehow sensed that Grammy would know he was lying.

Max then noticed something that made his skin crawl.

A black patch.

Over Grammy's left eye.

"You—you were the one I stabbed in the woods last night?" Max said, realizing that Grammy's need for bed rest wasn't because of a migraine.

Grammy nodded and patted the silver dagger tucked into the belt around her apron.

"Don't worry, dear. My eye will heal back to normal in no time. Werewolves don't stay wounded for long." She paused. "And I see you recovered your father's red hoodie. Ah well, it's no use now—the third night of the full moon is here."

Max's head spun with questions. Everything in him told him to run, but he was paralyzed with fear.

"You and Gramps are—are *both* werewolves?" he asked. "H-have you always been this way?"

Grammy stepped forward.

"There will be plenty of time for explanations," she said. "We're just glad you decided to come back to the cabin before the full moon reaches its peak."

"W-why?" Max asked, petrified that they might eat him.

Grammy leaned down and peered at him with her one good eye.

"Because you're just in time for your big surprise," she whispered.

23

THE BOY WHO CRIED WEREWOLF

They've been planning to eat me the whole time! Max thought.

Just then, Gramps walked out of the cabin. He looked at Max, relieved, but said nothing.

The old man made his way over to Grammy, and the two of them peered up at the sky together. The full moon had just reached its peak, and moonlight spilled over the forest like a beam from a flying saucer.

It slowly crept across the earth and into the nearby field.

Chasing after Max.

Closer.

And closer.

As soon as the moonlight touched Max, a sensation like fire burned through him.

He fell to his knees. And crumpled over.

"What's—happening?" he choked out in agony.

Gramps and Grammy remained silent. Observant. And knowing.

Max felt his blood searing through his veins like lava. His insides shifted, causing him to twist and turn. It felt like something inside him was trying to claw its way out. His vision became blurry, then sharp again, then sharper.

He looked down in terror. Hair spurted out of his pores, covering his arms and hands.

His teeth sharpened like razors.

His entire face and body became unrecognizable with fur.

He looked up and saw the blood-red moon hanging above him.

Then a monstrous howl rose from his chest and filled the night, invading every pocket of the forest.

"A-RRR-OOOOO!"

I'm a werewolf! he thought in terror.

A cacophony of sounds invaded his ears. He could hear the heartbeats of a thousand creatures hidden in the darkness!

His vision sharpened further until he could actually see all of them—owls, rabbits, mice, squirrels.

I have night vision!

He then discovered that his nose had turned into a grotesque snout that could smell everything from the leaves of the forest to Grammy's ambrosia-scented perfume. It was like having superpowers.

And the hunger! Oh, that ferocious pang of hunger! It ruled him. All those creatures he could hear, see, and smell, he now wanted to *taste*.

And then . . .

He tried to say something.

But no words escaped his lips.

All he could hear were his own grunts and . . .

Barking?

Max felt trapped inside his new form, like an astronaut sealed inside a space suit.

He looked up at Gramps and Grammy for answers.

"Werewolves can't speak when in wolf form," Gramps explained, still his human self. "But we can communicate through our thoughts. It's a wolf telepathy we inherited when one of our ancestors was bitten by a wolf in the eastern forest over a hundred years ago."

Am I dreaming? Is this a nightmare? Max wondered.

"You're not dreaming," Gramps assured him, reading Max's mind. "You were born this way. Just like us. Just like your father."

Max thought of the stuffed werewolf standing next to the window in the hermit's shack. A grim epiphany struck him like a lightning bolt . . .

Was my father the original beast all the towns-people were afraid of?!

Grammy sighed.

"What you've heard are mostly schoolyard tales," she said, studying his thoughts. "It's our code not to harm humans. The wolves of the eastern forest did kill a few sheep and hogs to feed their families, but only because much of their hunting grounds had been plundered by hunters. The real reason the population of Wolf County dwindled is because people started moving away to the cities—where everything is more convenient. Farmers are a dying breed nowadays."

But why has this all been kept a secret from me? he wondered, overwhelmed by the wild-ness within.

"Because you weren't ready for the truth," Grammy said. "We—and your mother—wanted you to have as normal a life as possible up until your first transformation. Once she informed us that you'd been showing the Signs—hearing things that no human should hear, smelling scents from a mile away, and catching falling items before they hit the ground—we sent your dad's red hoodie with the silver zipper to help suppress the beast within you until you could get here. And we put the dagger beside your bed for the same reason. We couldn't be sure that you were fully one of us until tonight—the third night of the full moon after your twelfth birthday."

I don't understand. What about everything I've seen? Max wondered. *The chickens? The muddy prints in my room? And the dog next door?*

"You had your first spell a couple nights ago," Grammy explained. "Eating chickens and rabbits. Attacking the dog next door. The muddy prints in your bedroom were your own from when you went sleep-hunting in the woods. That's why we locked you up in your room last night so that your scent couldn't be tracked."

Tracked? By who?

"By the monsters," she explained.

"That's what we call the hunters," Gramps

added, then stepped forward. "This may be hard for you to hear, Max, but I think it's time we finally tell you what really happened to your dad."

24

THE TRUTH

"As soon as you were born, your father began thinking about what kind of life you were going to have," Gramps said. "He didn't want you to have to go through the same things he did—always being hunted and always having to hide who you truly are. So he moved you and your mom out here to the farm, set up a small lab in the basement, and began searching for a cure."

A cure? Max thought, finding it hard to concentrate because of his new growling hunger.

The old man nodded. "He knew that silver

repelled wolf blood, so he began a series of experiments based on that hypothesis. At first, he tinkered with simple inventions like making a silver zipper for his favorite hoodie and crafting a silver dagger that would restrain the beast within. But those were merely temporary suppressors—your dad soon found a way to be rid of the wolf once and for all."

Gramps reached into his overalls pocket and pulled out a small vial. A bright silver liquid glowed within it.

Is that . . . Liquid Silver? Max telepathized.

"Found the blueprints in the cellar, did you?" Grammy interjected. "When you drink this, the silver absorbs into your bloodstream and dissolves the wolf blood in your veins. He offered it to your gramps and me, but wolf blood is all we've known our entire lives and we're settled in our ways. Your father wanted you to have a choice."

But how—how did he die?

Gramps sighed and peered deep into Max's yellow eyes.

"One stormy October night—Halloween, in fact—your father went into the forest to gather the last samples for his experiment. He needed pure wolf blood to run his tests, and the wolves in the eastern forest had been helping him. But that same night, the hunters swarmed the forest to finish off the wolves. Your father died trying to protect them—they were his family too, you know. He was able to help lead quite a few of them to safety before the hunters shot him."

Max's head spun with questions.

Was Mr. Howler the one who shot my father?

"No one knows what gun killed your father," Grammy said. "But when Mr. Howler heard your howls two nights ago, he tracked your paw prints into the forest with the intention of killing you. We knew he was on your trail—and we couldn't let him figure out that you were the beast—so we had to capture him and the girl last night while they were eating dinner. We couldn't risk him tracking your scent during the full moon or you attacking them during one of your spells."

So Jade knows everything too?

"She does now," Grammy continued. "We locked them both up in the cellar until the full moon passed—just to be safe. Their dog too. Don't worry, though—you can talk to Jade tomorrow morning after the sun comes up. She's still a bit in shock from the news that we're all werewolves. The good news is that she's doing everything she can to convince her father to make peace with our kind—Grammy and I both agree that she can be trusted."

Max thought of Jade, wondering what she was thinking at that very moment. He was thankful that she was trying to protect them, but he wondered whether she would still be his friend after the full moon had passed.

You don't think Mr. Howler will still come after us once you release him?

"Just to be safe, we'll give him a healthy dose of your father's amnesia powder," Grammy said, holding up a clear plastic container filled with what looked like purple baking flour.

"Wouldn't be the first time we've had to use

it on him," Gramps added with a wink. "But more important is this . . ."

Gramps held up the vial of Liquid Silver into the moonlight. It looked like it came from another world.

Max stared at the potion. All he had to do was drink it, and he could wake up from this nightmare.

Right then, Gramps cleared his throat, breaking Max's trance.

"Before you make your final decision," he said. "It's important that you know that wolf blood can be more of a gift than a curse. You'll be able to do things other humans can only dream of."

Max considered the possibilities. He could try out for the football team, the basketball team, even track! Maybe he could get a college scholarship and play pro ball someday. But he would always have to hide his true identity.

He looked down at his paws and then up at the bright candle in the sky. He thought of the hundreds of moons upon which he would have to keep his secret, and he wondered if it would all be worth it. It would be so easy to drink the potion and make the burden go away forever.

Then he remembered the ache he had felt all his life. The ache of not knowing who his father was. Of not having any sort of connection with him. He recalled how lonely and lost he had felt his entire life.

And his decision became as clear as day.

I—I don't want to be cured, he communicated to Gramps and Grammy. *The blood in my veins is all I have left of my dad. If being a werewolf makes me more like him, then that's what I want.*

Gramps and Grammy exchanged a surprised look.

"If that's your wish, boy, then we'll honor it," Grammy said. "Just always know, the cure is here if you ever change your mind."

Max stepped toward Gramps. He took the vial of Liquid Silver into his palms. It felt warm and alive. Without a second thought, he threw the vial to the ground and shattered it. The potion spilled, glowing eerily for a moment, then melted into the earth.

I won't need it. Max smiled. *This is who I am.*

Gramps beamed with pride.

"There is something else we wanted to give you," the old man said, reaching into his overalls pocket. "It's a birthday present from your dad. He left it for you."

Max squinted in confusion.

What is it?

"Your father's silver compass," Gramps explained. "It was his prized possession, a family heirloom passed down through generations of Bloodnights. My father gave it to me when I was your age, and I gave it to your father."

Max admired the ancient moon cycles upon its face.

"Your dad called this his good luck charm. He always carried it with him . . . except on the night he died. As he was leaving the house, he said he had a strange feeling, and he gave the compass to me to give to you should something happen to him."

Max took the silver compass and turned it over. The inscription on the back read:

For Max.
On his 12th Birthday.
I'm Always with You.
Love,
Dad

Max's heart overflowed with warmth. He was speechless. It was the first tangible gift he had ever received from his father.

This is the best birthday present ever, Max thought, his fangs glimmering in the moonlight like tiny stars.

He gazed down at the compass and then up at Gramps and Grammy.

And for the first time in his life, Max didn't feel so alone.

25

A PERFECT COSTUME

The next morning, Max awoke at the rooster's crow.

He looked down at his hands and saw that they were no longer furry paws. He felt his teeth and was glad to discover that they were no longer fangs. After examining his normal self, he wondered if the night before had all been a dream.

When Max arrived downstairs, no one was there.

He stepped onto the front porch and saw Gramps at the edge of the pumpkin patch, digging a large hole with a shovel.

Max ran over to him.

"Your father has deserved a proper burial for some time. We never knew where his body was until you told us of your discovery last night. What do you say we go get it?"

Max nodded reverently.

It wasn't a dream after all, he thought, reaching into his pocket and feeling the silver compass.

The two of them walked together deep into woods and toward the shack. They wrapped Max's father's body in one of Grammy's patchwork quilts, and carried it together, hardly saying a word the entire way back to the farm.

After they finished burying him, Max picked up a handful of dirt, and let it sift through his fingers onto his father's grave. A tear ran down his cheek, and he felt a strange satisfaction like that of closing a book after reading the last page.

"I wish I didn't have to leave," Max admitted.

"You can come back anytime you want,"

Gramps assured him, patting Max's shoulder. "Think of this place as your home away from home."

Max stared at the ground, deep in thought.

"I'm kind of nervous about going back to school. I mean, how do I control my transformations?"

Gramps chuckled slightly, as if he understood the question all too well.

"They'll be a little tricky at first, but you'll get the hang of it. Eventually, when you feel your blood starting to boil, you'll be able to control it," Gramps said. "In the meantime, just make sure you wear that hoodie for another few moon cycles until you get the hang of things."

"So there's nothing else I need to know? No training or guidelines or rules?"

Gramps stared at the ground for a long moment, scratching his chin.

"Well, for starters, always wear lots of cologne. Even if you shower three times a day, you're going to smell like you just crawled out of the swamp. And hide some mouthwash in your backpack during school. You don't want to have wolf breath when you're talking to a girl. Also, always keep a comb in your back pocket. Whenever you turn back into your human form after a transformation, your hair is going to be a mess. Floss every day, no exceptions. You only get one set o' fangs. Most important—perhaps most important of all—only talk about werewolf things to other werewolves. We haven't existed in secret for this long without extreme caution. If certain people ever found out about us, it could be dangerous to our entire kind."

"You mean there are other werewolves out there besides us?"

But Gramps didn't answer.

Max thought about this for a moment. He wished Gramps could always be there to teach him the things he needed to know.

"Gramps, do you think maybe you and Grammy could get a cell phone? You know, just so I can call and talk to you sometimes," he asked, already missing his new family. "They have solar chargers now, so you still wouldn't have to get electricity."

Gramps grimaced at the idea, but then he let out a sigh of surrender.

"I think we might be able to make a small compromise for our grandson," he said, then tousled Max's hair. "Say, looks like you have a visitor."

Gramps started toward the house, and Max turned to see Jade approaching him. He wasn't sure what she thought of him now.

"So," she finally said. "You're a ... werewolf."

Max nodded, afraid of what she might say next.

"Pretty cool," she said.

Max smiled.

"Listen," Jade continued. "I wrote down my mailing address. You should write to me sometimes. I promise to write back."

She handed him a folded piece of notebook paper. He glanced down at it, then put it in his pocket.

"Thanks, Jade. I'm really glad that we met. And I'm even more glad that you weren't eaten by one of us," he said.

"Hey, the full moon comes once a month, so there's still time," she teased. "You'll be coming back, won't you?"

"I hope so," Max said. "I mean . . . you can count on it."

He was glad to have a friend who knew his secret. Someone he could trust. And be himself around.

"Looks like your mom is here," Jade said, pointing to a blue minivan driving up the dirt road. A cloud of dust hovered in its wake.

Max turned.

"Yeah, I better get packed up," he said. "See you soon?"

"Definitely," she said, then skipped away through the pumpkin patch and back to her house, where her father was harvesting the final pumpkins of the year.

Max's mom pulled up in front of the cabin and stepped out of the van. She approached Grammy, who was setting out a freshly carved jack-o'-lantern on the front porch. Max noticed that the old woman's eye was back to normal, just like she said it would be.

"It's good to see he's taken to this place," Max's mother said to Grammy.

"The boy's one of us, all right," Grammy said with a smile.

Just then, Max ran up and hugged his mom.

She hugged him back, surprised to find him in such high spirits.

"Mom, is it all right if we stay for lunch? Grammy's making barbecue," he pleaded.

"But you don't eat meat," she said in surprise.

Max shrugged.

"Things change," he said with a playful grin.

Max's mother looked at Grammy questioningly.

"And Mom?" Max said softly. "I know what happened to Dad. I'm—I'm really sorry. I know it's been just as hard for you as it has been for me. In different ways."

She looked at him thoughtfully. Tears reflected in her eyes, and the sadness on her face turned to relief.

"Oh, but son, your father never left us. I see him in you every day," she said, then leaned down and kissed Max's forehead.

They hugged for a long moment.

"Someday, remind me to tell you about how I met your father," she added wistfully.

"I thought you met in college," Max said.

"That's only half the story. Your mother has secrets too, you know," she said with a wink. And for a moment, Max thought he saw slim fangs hiding behind her rosy lips. He suddenly remembered what Gramps had said about there being other werewolves in the world. But he decided it was just his imagination. "Oh, and I brought a charger for your iPad so you can play games in the car on the way home."

"Thanks, Mom," he replied. "But I think I'll wait to play it once we get back to the house. I don't want to miss the view."

She looked down at him in surprise, then put her arm around him. Gramps joined them on the porch, and all four of them walked toward the front door of the cabin.

Just before they stepped inside, Max's mother added, "By the way . . . have you figured out what you're going to be for Halloween yet? It's your last year to go trick-or-treating, you know."

Max looked up at Gramps and Grammy, then back to his mother.

"I think I have something in mind," he said with a mischievous grin.

And for the rest of the morning and the entire drive home, he practiced turning his hands into paws, deciding that he would be able to go trick-or-treating every Halloween for the rest of his life.

ACKNOWLEDGMENTS

"I am a part of all that I have met."
—Alfred, Lord Tennyson

There are quite a few people to acknowledge here in this first book of the Monsterstreet series:

First of all, my Mom, Dad, Sis—everything I am is because of you, and words can never express the depth of my gratefulness. I can only hope to honor you with the life I live and the works I create.

All my family: Granddad, Grandmom, Pappa Hugg, Mamma Hugg, Lilla, Meemaw, Nanny, GG, Grandmother Hugghins, Marilyn, Steve, Haddie, Jude, Beckett, Uncle Hal, Aunt

Cathy, Nicole, Dylan, Aunt Rhonda, Uncle Greg, Sam, Jake, Trey, Uncle Johnny, Aunt Glynis, Jerod, Chad, Aunt Jodie, Uncle Terry, Natalie, Mitchell, Anna, David, Hannah, David Nevin, Joy, Lukas, Teresa, and Aunt Jan.

Teachers, coaches, mentors, colleagues, and students: Jeanie Johnson, David Vardeman, Pat Vaughn, Lee Carter, Robert Darden, Kevin Reynolds, Ray Bradbury, R.L. Stine, Rikki Coke (Wiethorn), Peggy Jezek, Kathi Couch, Jill Osborne Wilkinson, Marla Jaynes, Karen Deaconson, Su Milam, Karen Copeland, Corrie Dixon, Nancy Evans Hutto, Pam Dominik, Jean Garner, Randy Crawford, Pat Zachry, Eddie Sherman, Scott Copeland, Heidi Kunkel, Brian Boyd, Sherry Rogers, Lisa Osborne, Wes Evans, Betsy Barry, Karen Hix, Sherron Boyd, Mrs. Kahn, Mrs. Turk, Mrs. Schroeder, Mrs. Battle, Mrs. McCracken, Nancy Frame Chiles, Mrs. Adkins, Kim Pearson, Mrs. Harvey, Elaine Spence, Barbara Fulmer, Julie Schrotel, Barbara Belk, Mrs. Reynolds, Vanessa Diffenbaugh, Elisabeth McKetta, Bryan Delaney,

Talaya Delaney, Wendy Allman, John Belew, Vicki Klaras, Gery Greer and Bob Ruddick, Greg Garrett, Chris Seay, Sealy and Matt Yates, David Crowder, Cecile Goyette, Kirby Kim, Mike Simpson, Quinlan Lee, Clay Butler, Mary Darden, Derek Smith, Brian Elliot, Rachel Moore, Naymond Keathley, Steve Sadler, Jimmy and Janet Dorrell, Glenn Blalock, Katie Cook, SJ Murray, Greg Chan, Lorri Shackelford, Tim Fleischer, Byron Weathersbee, Chuck Walker, John Durham, Ron Durham, Bob Johns, Kyle Lake, Kevin Roe, Barby Williams, Nancy Parrish, Joani Livingston, Madeleine Barnett, Diane McDaniel, Beth Hair, Laura Cubos, Sarah Holland, Christe Hancock, Cheryl Cooper, Jeni Smith, Traci Marlin, Jeremy Ferrerro, Maurice and Gloria Walker, Charlotte McDonald, Dana Gietzen, Leighanne Parrish, Heather Helton, Corrie Cubos, all the librarians, teachers, secretaries, students, custodians, and principals at Midway ISD, Waco ISD, Riesel ISD, and Connally ISD, all my apprentices at Moonsung Writing Camp and Camp Imagination, and to my hometown community of Woodway, Texas.

Friends and collaborators: Nathan "Waylon" Jennings, Craig Cunningham, Blake Graham, Susannah Lipsey, Hallie Day, Ali Rodman Wallace, Jered Wilkerson, Brian McDaniel, Meghan Stanley Lynd, Suzanne Hoag Steece, the Jennings family, the Rodman family, the Carter family, all the families of the "Red River Gang," the Cackleberries, the Geib family, Neva Walker and family, Rinky and Hugh Sanders, Clay Rodman, Steven Fischer, Dustin Boyd, Jeff Vander Woude, Randy Stephens, Allen Ferguson, Scott Lynd, Josh Zachry, Scott Crawford, Jourdan Gibson Stewart, Crystal Carter, Kristi Kangas Miller, Taylor Christian, Deanna Dyer Williams, Matt Jennings, Laurie McCool Henderson, Trey Witcher, Genny Pattillo Davis, Brady Williams, Brook Williams Henry, Michael Henry, Jamie Jennings, Jordan Jones, Adrianna Bell Walker, Sarah Rogers Combs, Kayleigh Cunningham, Rich and Megan Roush, Adam Chop, Kimberly Garth

Batson, Luke Stanton, Kevin Brown, Britt
Knighton, George Cowden, Jenny and Ryan
Jamison, Julie Hamilton, Kyle and Emily
Knighton, Ray Small, Jeremy Combs, Mike
Trozzo, Allan Marshall, Coleman Hampton,
Kent Rabalais, Laura Aldridge, Mikel Hatfield
Porter, Edith Reitmeier, Ben Geib, Ashley
Vandiver Dalton, Tamarah Johnson, Amanda
Hutchison Thompson, Morgan McKenzie
Williams, Robbie Phillips, Shane Wilson, J.R.
Fleming, Andy Dollerson, Terry Anderson,
Mary Anzalone, Chris Ermoian, Chris Erlanson,
Greg Peters, Doreen Ravenscroft, Brooke
Larue Miceli, Emily Spradling Freeman,
Brittany Braden Rowan, Kim Evans Young,
Kellis Gilleland Webb, Lindsay Crawford,
April Carroll Mureen, Rebekah Croft Georges,
Amanda Finnell Brown, Kristen Rash Di
Campli, Clint Sherman, Big Shane Smith, Little
Shane Smith, Allen Childs, Brandon Hodges,
Justin Martin, Eric Lovett, Cody Fredenberg,
Tierre Simmons, Bear King, Brady Lillard,

Charlie Collier, Aaron Hattier, Keith Jordan, Greg Weghorst, Seth Payne, BJ Carr, Andria Mullins Scarbrough, Lindsey Kelley Palumbo, Cayce Connell Bellinger, David Maness, Ryan Smith, Marc Uptmore, Kelly Maddux McCarver, Robyn Klatt Areheart, Emily Hoyt Crew, Matt Etter, Logan Walter, Jessica Talley, JT Carpenter, Ryan Michaelis, Audrey Malone Andrews, Amy Achor Blankson, Chad Conine, Hart Robinson, Wade Washmon, Clay Gibson, Barrett Hall, Chad Lemons, Les Strech, Marcus Dracos, Tyler Ellis, Taylor Rudd, James Yarborough, Scott Robison, Bert Vandiver, Clark Richardson, Luke Blount, Allan Gipe, Daniel Fahlenkamp, Ben Hogan, Chris Porter, Reid Johnson, Ryan Stanton, Brian Reis, Ty Sprague, Eric Ellis, Jeremy Gann, Jeff Sadler, Ryan Pryor, Jared Ray, Dustin Dickerson, Reed Collins, Ben Marx, Sammy Rajaratnam, Art Wellborn, Cory Ferguson, Jonathan King, Jim King, Anthony Edwards, Craig Nash, Dillon Meek, Jonathan Stringer, the Bode and Moore families, Jackie and Denver Mills, the Warrior

Poets, the Wild Hearts, the Barbaric Yawps, the Bangarang Brothers, and all the Sacred Circle guys (CARPE DIEM).

To all the writers, directors, composers, producers, artists, creators, inventors, poets, and thinkers who have shaped my life, work, and imagination—a list of luminaries which is far too long to mention here.

To Chris Fenoglio, for creating such stunning covers for the Monsterstreet series. It's safe to say your illustrations pass the ultimate test: they would have made me want to pick up the books when I was a boy! Thank you for lending your incredible talent and imagination to this project.

To the Stimola Literary Studio Family: Erica Rand Silverman, Adriana Stimola, Peter Ryan, Allison Remcheck, and all my fellow authors who are lucky enough to call the Stimola Literary Studio their home.

To the entire HarperCollins publishing family and Katherine Tegen family: Katherine Tegen, David Curtis, Erin Fitzsimmons, Jon

Howard, Robby Imfeld, Haley George, and Tanu Srivastava.

To my amazing agent, Rosemary Stimola, who plucked me out of obscurity, remained faithful to this project over the course of not just months but years, and who sets the highest standard of integrity within the wondrous world of children's publishing. I can't tell you how deeply grateful I am for all that you have done for me.

And to my extraordinary editor, Ben Rosenthal. From our very first conversation reminiscing about 1980s movies, I felt in my gut that you were a kindred spirit. Our collaboration on the Monsterstreet series has been one of the greatest joys and adventures of my life, and it's an enormous honor to get to share this journey with you. Thank you for all your guidance, encouragement, and optimism along the way . . . you've been a fantastic captain of this ship!

To my wife and best friend, Rebekah . . . no words can ever tell you how grateful I am for the thousands of hours you've spent reading rough drafts, listening to unpolished ideas, and offering warm, thoughtful encouragement every step of the way. These books wouldn't exist without you, and I'm so glad I get to share this journey and all others by your side.

And lastly, to my most cherished treasures, my precious daughters, Lily Belle and Poet Eve: it is the greatest joy of my life to watch you gaze upon the world with wonder and tell us what you see. May stories always enchant you, and may you tell your own stories someday.

KEEP READING FOR A SNEAK PEEK AT ANOTHER
CHILLING MONSTERSTREET ADVENTURE

1

THE HOUSE AT THE END OF MAPLE STREET

Fisher gripped the straps of his backpack as he trudged down Maple Street, gazing in each window at the silhouettes of boys and girls putting on homemade costumes and nibbling on fresh-baked treats. Jack-o'-lanterns grinned at him from cobwebbed porches. Blow-up monsters and plastic gravestones loomed on leaf-covered lawns. And the sugary scent of candy wafted through the crisp autumn air, enchanting his nostrils. It seemed every house on the block was decorated for Halloween.

All except one.

The house at the end of Maple Street looked just as ordinary as it did on any other day of the year. There wasn't a single pumpkin, not one fake spider, not even a sign that greeted guests with *Happy Halloween!*

Fisher walked up to the door of the house, turned the brass knob, and stepped inside. He reached down to pet his cat, and heard his mom's voice echoing from the kitchen. . . .

". . . Yes, I accept the position. We'll be there before Thanksgiving. I'm very much looking forward to this opportunity."

Fisher peeked around the corner just as his mom hung up the phone. She was wearing jeans and a sweater, and her short brown hair looked darker in the shadows where she sat.

"Who was that?" Fisher asked.

His mom winced, startled. "No one."

"It had to be someone," Fisher pried.

His mom sighed.

"If you must know, I was offered a vice principal position in that town on the coast I was telling you about."

"We're moving . . . again?" Fisher's voice reeked of disappointment.

"You know how much I don't like being here," his mom said. "I lived in this town, and in this house, long enough while I was growing up. I told you when we moved this summer that it was only a temporary stop for you and me after the divorce—until we could get settled somewhere better."

"But I'm just starting to get used to this place," Fisher said. "Some guys at school even asked me to go trick-or-treating with them tonight. Do you know how hard it is to get invited to something at a new school? Everyone's had the same friends since kindergarten."

"You can make new friends after we move," his mom replied.

"That's what you said last time, and so that's what I'm trying to do," Fisher pointed out.

"There's no negotiating on this," his mom said.

Fisher felt the hot fire of anger burning in his chest, and he tried to push it down deep where he kept all his feelings. But it was too much to hold in.

"If you and Dad hadn't gotten a divorce, I never would have had to leave my friends in the first place!" he erupted like a volcano.

His mom was silent. Fisher knew mentioning the divorce was a powerful weapon, and he only used it when he felt he had no other choice.

"You're entitled to your own feelings about it. And so am I," his mom said, but her words felt cold. Like she wasn't listening to him. Ever since the divorce, he felt like he and his mom were living on two different planets with nothing in common but their last name.

"Why do you have to be so selfish?" Fisher mumbled.

"What did you say?"

Fisher debated whether to say it again. Instead, he said something worse.

"Dad wouldn't make me move again."

He saw the color of anger fill his mom's face.

"Well, your dad isn't here, is he? And as

long as you're living under my roof, you'll live by my rules."

"I hate your rules!" Fisher shouted, still unable to control his temper.

"That's it, young man. You're grounded," she said in her principal-like voice.

"But what about Halloween?"

"Doesn't make any difference to me what day it is," she returned. "You know I don't care for Halloween anyway."

"But Mom!"

"With that attitude, you can stay in your room for the entire weekend. I've already put some moving boxes upstairs, so you can get an early start on packing."

"That's not fair!"

"Okay. The next month! Keep it up and you'll be grounded for the rest of sixth grade."

He stared at her for a long moment, then decided arguing would only make things worse. He turned and walked up the stairs to his bedroom and lay down in his reading tent, where he kept his stash of comic books and monster figurines.

He heard his mom shout from downstairs, "By the way, I have to chaperone the Halloween dance at the high school later, so I'll bring your dinner up before I leave. And no TV while I'm gone—I don't want you having nightmares from all those monster movies that will be on tonight!"

Fisher glanced across the room to the pile of cardboard boxes waiting to be filled. He had just unpacked everything a few months before, and now his mom was making him do it all again.

Why can't Mom just listen to me for once? And why can't she just let me go trick-or-treating?

Right then, a staticky sound buzzed over the walkie-talkie in his backpack.

A boy's raspy voice came through. "The meeting's about to start. You coming or what?"

2

SECRET HIDEOUT

Fisher ripped the white sheet from his bed and used his pocketknife to cut out two oval holes for his eyes.

"This will have to do for my costume," he whispered, tucking the ghost sheet into his backpack and climbing out the window.

As soon as his feet hit the ground, he ran to his bike. Then he pedaled as fast as he could into the forest at the edge of the neighborhood, just as the boy on the walkie-talkie had told him to do.

The afternoon sun beamed through the

skeleton trees, bathing the woods with an eerie autumn glow. Red and brown leaves crunched beneath his tires as he passed an old graveyard, running his fingers over the spikes of the rusted iron fence. A hundred yards up, he arrived at a giant oak tree three times the size of any others in sight. Its limbs were gnarled, twisted, and full of knots. A deep hollow stared out from its trunk like the eye socket of a skull.

Fisher saw three other bikes lying on the ground near the base of the tree, and he knew he was in the right place.

High above, a tree house was cradled within its limbs, hidden in camouflage.

A handmade wooden sign hung on its side:

THE HALLOWEENERS
Est. 1955